Burning air seared Darcy's lungs.

She'd woken up tied to a wooden chair in a basement, with a taste like burned sugar in her mouth. The fog of confusion swamped her brain. To her right, the stairs were ablaze in flames so bright they stung her eyes. Her only exit was through fire.

She was trapped.

"Help me!" she screamed.

How did she get here? She could feel the pull of unconsciousness dragging at the edges of her mind, tempting her to give in and pass out again. Darcy rocked back and forth in her chair, thrashing against her bonds.

"Lucas!" she called.

She rocked harder, hoping to break herself free. The smoke was now so thick she could barely see. Then the stairs collapsed completely, caving in on themselves in a thunderous crash.

Help me, God. I'm not going to make it.

A dog barked and Darcy shifted to see a flash of golden fur leaping toward her through the flames.

"Hold on, Darcy!" Lucas's strong voice reached her through the panic. "I'm coming!"

Maggie K. Black is an award-winning journalist and romantic suspense author with an insatiable love of traveling the world. She has lived in the American South, Europe and the Middle East. She now makes her home in Canada with her history-teacher husband, their two beautiful girls and a small but mighty dog.

Books by Maggie K. Black

Love Inspired Suspense

Undercover Protection
Surviving the Wilderness
Her Forgotten Life
Cold Case Chase
Undercover Baby Rescue

Mountain Country K-9 Unit

Crime Scene Secrets

Unsolved Case Files

Cold Case Tracker
Christmas Cold Case
Dangerous Arson Trail

Visit the Author Profile page at LoveInspired.com for more titles.

DANGEROUS ARSON TRAIL

MAGGIE K. BLACK

LOVE INSPIRED SUSPENSE
INSPIRATIONAL ROMANCE

LOVE INSPIRED® SUSPENSE
INSPIRATIONAL ROMANCE

ISBN-13: 978-1-335-98056-4

Recycling programs
for this product may
not exist in your area.

Dangerous Arson Trail

Love Inspired
22 Adelaide St. West, 41st Floor
Toronto, Ontario M5H 4E3, Canada
www.LoveInspired.com

Printed in U.S.A.

Behold, how great a matter a little fire kindleth!
And the tongue is a fire.
—*James* 3:5–6

To everyone I've hurt with thoughtless words, lost my temper at and said stupid things to when I was younger.

Especially those I don't even remember burning.

I'm sorry.

ONE

Chaotic and panicked screams filled Darcy Lane's 911 headset. In the small town of Sunset, north of Toronto, a group of teenagers had been skipping school and playing video games together when a boy named Carter had suddenly collapsed. A map on the screen in front of her told Darcy that the paramedics she'd dispatched were less than two minutes away.

Right now, it was a matter of keeping everyone calm, getting the information paramedics needed and making sure the sick kid was okay until help could get to him.

Every second was critical.

Lord, help me to help them...

"It's going to be okay." Darcy kept her voice steady, level and reassuring, without even allowing a hint of her own worry or concern slip through. "Help is on its way. Is Carter conscious?"

"I... I..." The girl gasped a shallow breath. "I don't know. I can't tell."

"Are his eyes open?"

"They're kind of fluttering."

Which meant he was breathing. *Thank You, God.* Darcy typed the information into her keyboard to inform paramedics.

"You're doing great," Darcy told her. "Ambulances are almost there. Just take a deep breath in and out for me. What's your name?"

"Brittany." Pain laced the teenager's voice. "Tell them to hurry. He's my boyfriend, and he's bleeding a lot."

Darcy's heart lurched. At twenty-four, she was only a few years older than the girl on the phone and couldn't imagine how panicked she must be. Not that she'd had a boyfriend at that age—unless she counted the fleeting few hours after Lucas Harper had kissed her. Then he'd told her he had made a mistake, ended their short-lived romance, effectively torpedoed their friendship and abruptly moved to the other side of the country. Two years older than she was, with green eyes, a shy, quiet smile, and an incredibly good heart, Lucas had been the boy next door. He'd been her favorite person and her secret crush all rolled into one for as long as she could remember. They'd grown up in Sunset, on the southernmost edge of Lake Simcoe. According to town gossip, Lucas was now a K-9 cop with Ontario's newly formed Cold Case Task Force.

Back then, if she'd ever seen Lucas collapse, she'd have wanted to throw him over her shoulder and take him to the hospital herself. As well as call in every law enforcement officer and paramedic she could.

"They're almost there," Darcy said, "and you're doing great. Right now, I need you to focus. Do you know if Carter consumed any drugs or alcohol?"

"We just got jobs…" Brittany hesitated. "At the drive-in."

And no doubt whatever she thought her boyfriend had taken could cost him that job.

"Look, this is not about getting anyone in trouble," Darcy said and leaned forward. "Paramedics need to know what he took in order to help him."

"I… I think he takes pills, but I don't know what they are."

Darcy typed furiously. "What color are they?"

"Blue."

Then Darcy heard the sounds of sirens and fresh voices down the line. Her screen told her that paramedics and police had arrived. Still, she waited to hear the voice of an officer on the line, assuring her that they'd taken over the scene.

As Darcy hung up, the sounds of other voices taking calls and fingers typing buzzed at the edge of her consciousness. The regional 911 center was on the second floor of a sprawling glass-and-concrete police building on the northernmost edge of the Toronto area. Rows of dispatchers sat at plain gray desks in front of large flat-screened computers, taking calls from dozens of small towns and suburbs in the surrounding area. The clock told her it was a quarter to three in the afternoon. She allowed herself one deep breath and another quick prayer for all those involved in the drive-in incident; then she pressed a button and focused all her attention on the next person who needed her help.

"911," Darcy said. "Police, fire or ambulance?"

There was no answer. An odd static crackled down the line.

"Hello, 911? What is your emergency?"

Again, no answer.

Almost a quarter of the calls Darcy and her fellow dispatchers received were accidental dials, pranks or nuisance calls. But still, she had a duty to treat each one as a potential life-or-death situation until she knew otherwise. She glanced at the screen again, hoping to see the caller's GPS location pinpointed on her map. But the call was untraceable.

"Hello?" she tried again.

"Hellllo, hoooney." The voice was cold, male and distorted.

"Are you ready to have a fun and fabulous time?"

A crank call, obviously. She was a second away from rolling her eyes and terminating it when the voice began to laugh, and something about the mocking tone... It seemed to almost drip down the line into Darcy's ears, tugging out terrifying memories of the past.

No! It can't be!

She sat up straight, her teeth set on edge in anger. Eight years since an arsonist had used that very same distorted tone to terrorize Sunset. Countless mimics had tried to prank 911 with it since.

"You're pretending to be Blaze?" Her voice rose. "Do you get how sick and inappropriate that is?"

Professionally, she knew she shouldn't have said any of that. But she couldn't help herself. She'd been sixteen when a classmate of hers named Robby Lamb had created a persona called Blaze. He'd used it to set four buildings on fire, kill a security guard and post terrifying videos online of a hooded figure threatening to burn her community to the ground. But he'd been caught, and then confessed. It was Darcy herself who'd figured out that Robby was the culprit. But now Robby was dead. He'd passed away in a fire while out on bond for his crimes.

Laughter cackled down the line. She steeled a breath and asked God to help her regain her focus. She had a job to do, and this had to be nothing more than a gross and disgusting prank.

"It's a crime to misuse emergency lines," she said. "Do you require police, fire or—"

"Listen to me!" Blaze's voice snapped with sudden ferocity. "We're going to play a trivia game and if you lose, people are going to die."

The blood froze in Darcy's veins, as a warning voice inside her shouted that this wasn't just a prankster.

Something about his tone of voice sounded different. This time, it was a threat.

"Get ready for an explosion, everybody," his menacing voice went on, "because we're going set the stage on fire. Tick tock, tick tock."

The line went dead.

"Hello?" Darcy clicked the button in a vain attempt to get him back. "Hello?"

He was gone, leaving nothing but the echo of his voice and a clammy shiver on her skin. What had just happened? Was it a prank? Was it a threat from a genuine copycat? The sounds of 911 dispatchers rose around her. Call lights blinked in front of her. Dozens of people were waiting for her help. Cranks happened every single day. Protocol was to brush it off and move on. But there'd been something about that voice she just couldn't shake.

Help me, Lord! What do I do?

She closed her eyes to pray, but memories of Robby began to spool out inside her thoughts. She'd known him from the school play—she'd been backstage crew, and Robby was one of the lead actors. They'd been in the same grade but hadn't been friends. Her suspicions had been based on a dozen tiny, little clues that had added up in her mind like a fragile tower of matchsticks—like the way Robby would play with his lighter or the way he'd practice doing odd voices when he thought no one was listening. She'd gone to Lucas, who had talked to his father, Fire Chief Ed Harper.

Ed had then spoken to Robby and somehow gotten the teen to confess and turn himself in—which would have been a happy ending to the whole situation if Robby hadn't then died in a fire, presumably by accident.

Blaze's voice still swam like dark eels at the edge of her consciousness, and suddenly one specific memory filled her mind. Five days before Robby had been arrested, she'd been manning the curtains when he bounded onto the stage in front of a packed gymnasium, picked up a microphone and introduced the Meadowvale High Spring Showcase with, "Get ready for an explosion, everybody, because we're going to set the stage on fire!"

Oh no... Had this new Blaze copycat just threatened to burn down the school?

Clarity moved through her veins and turned quickly into certainty. Her fingers hit the phone lines.

"To all available units," she said into her headset, "possible 10-62 arson threat at Meadowvale High School. Fire, police and ambulance respond. Again, 10-62 at Meadowvale High School. Perpetrator potentially using the identity of Blaze or a Blaze copycat. All available units respond."

She waited for confirmation from police, paramedics and firefighters that they were en route, then ended the call and prayed she hadn't solved the riddle too late.

Lord, please keep the students, staff and responders safe. May rescue get there in time!

"You've called in an all-hands response to an arson threat?" Supervisor Simon Phillips asked in his perpetually calm and unflappable voice. She hadn't even realized he was behind her. She turned. The 911 floor supervisor was lanky, bald and somewhere in his fifties. He scanned the screen as emergency vehicles converged on the school. "You said it was Blaze, as in Robby Lamb?"

"Yes," Darcy said. "Well, no. Because obviously Robby's dead. But it was somebody using the exact same voice distortion and way of talking. So I'm guessing it's a really good copycat."

Who'd done an unbelievably good job of mimicking the way Blaze talked.

The lines of Simon's forehead deepened. "And he called in an arson threat against the high school?"

"Well, it was a riddle," Darcy explained, "a quote from Robby's last school play, and I solved it."

Again, she was aware of the fact that they were surrounded in all directions by dozens and dozens of other 911 dispatchers.

What would've happened if one of them had taken the call instead of her? Would they have just dismissed it as a prank? She couldn't imagine any of them would've been able to solve the riddle.

"I'll review the call," her supervisor said. "It's also been passed on to the arson unit of the local police, who will have someone on-site at the school. And I'll contact Fire Chief Harper, as I'm sure he'll want to hear since he was part of the original case. Good job, Miss Lane."

"Thank you." Darcy nodded. Visions of kids running from the flames filled her mind, but she forced them aside, stilled her breath and reached to answer the next 911 call.

Lord, I have to do my job and leave this in Your hands...

For the next hour, she calmed panicked nerves, talked people through CPR, and dispatched police, firefighters and paramedics, all while silently praying that the high school would be evacuated safely and the new Blaze copycat would be caught.

As her shift neared its end, she looked up to see her supervisor walking toward her. He wasn't smiling, but she couldn't read anything in his face beyond that. Worry twisted knots inside her stomach.

"Is everything okay at the high school?" she asked and stood. "Did they get everyone out in time?"

"It was a false alarm," Simon said and frowned slightly.

"The school was evacuated, but no fire or incendiary devices were found."

"What?" Relief and confusion battled in her heart. But the school was the only logical answer to Blaze's riddle. Had she been wrong? Was he after another target?

"The arson unit is still investigating, right?" she asked.

"I suppose they will be," he said, "if they think a crime has been committed beyond a prank. But I also got Fire Chief Ed Harper to listen to the call. He said he didn't recognize the voice and was emphatic that it didn't sound at all like Blaze."

"No." Darcy shook her head. "That's not possible. The copycat's voice was so perfect…it was like it was the same guy."

"We get a few calls every year from pranksters pretending to be Blaze," Simon reminded her. "They all pretty much use the same voice trick. Some mimic it better than others. It's just a matter of using a voice modulator."

"I know." Frustration burned at back of her throat. "But this one felt different. He was angry. He was cruel. His way of talking was the same. It didn't sound like a prankster. He *sounded* like Blaze."

"In Ed's opinion, the call was a hoax," her supervisor replied. "He called the voice a bad imitation. The school trustees and principal are requesting more information about the call, considering it shut down the school and caused the cancellation of extracurriculars. They take hoaxes seriously because false alarms lead to complacency, which increases the risk of death in a real emergency."

Yeah, she knew. But this hadn't been a hoax.

"I'm putting together a joint press release with the fire department now," he went on, "basically saying that while the caller didn't make a specific threat against the school, one of our dispatchers sent emergency services out of an abundance of caution." Even if the press release didn't outright say the call was a hoax, it definitely implied that it was.

"They can't do that," Darcy said. "Ed is wrong. It was definitely Blaze's voice on the call, and people need to be warned they could be in danger."

"Based on what evidence?" Simon asked. "That the caller quoted a line that Robby Lamb said in a play eight years ago, which only a couple of hundred people who'd seen the play might even have a slim hope of remembering?"

Well, it did sound a little ridiculous when he said it like that. Even if she'd been wrong about the school and there was a different target, she was certain this couldn't be ignored.

"Well, then maybe the riddle wasn't actually meant to be solved!" Darcy gasped as the thought hit her like a literal punch to the gut. "Maybe he'd just planted it like a bread-crumb, to be deciphered by investigators when they reviewed the call after the school had burned down and teenagers died."

If so, Blaze's plan might've only been stopped because Darcy had been the one to take the call.

"I can see you feel strongly about this—" her supervisor's voice dropped "—but it sounds like you're grasping at straws. Even if I agreed with you, I don't have the authority to stop the fire department from issuing a press release. This is coming from the fire chief. Unfortunately, prank calls are part of the job, and you handled it the best you could." She could tell that he was trying to reassure her. But that was the last thing she wanted to hear right now. "I get the impression you're the kind of person who cares about things deeply. But you need to try to learn to let it go when the call is over and trust first responders to do their job. Otherwise, this might not be the right career fit for you."

But I'm right! Ed's wrong, and people are in danger!

The words flew across her mind, and she silently thanked God when she managed to catch them before they left her lips. Her supervisor might've been working for 911 a lot longer than she had, but he didn't have any more power to tell the fire chief what to do than she did.

Simon did however have the power to fire her.

Help me, Lord! How do I get people to take this new Blaze copycat seriously before people get hurt?

"It's almost the end of your shift," the supervisor added. "Why don't you take the rest of the day off and come back fresh tomorrow?"

She didn't exactly like the idea of leaving work early, but his tone made her wonder if she was at risk of skating on thin ice if she tried arguing with him any further. So Darcy took a deep breath, thanked him, logged off and clocked out from work.

Within minutes, Darcy was on the highway, heading north toward Sunset.

How dare her supervisor criticize her for caring about things deeply? Sure, she did. Sometimes. When it really mattered. But that didn't mean she was bad at her job. In fact, she'd gotten pretty good at turning the emotional tap off when she needed to.

The road was smooth beneath her tires. Beautiful farmland spread out on either side. But her chest still hurt so tightly that it stung with every breath. People could be in danger. Back in high school, Lucas had taken her seriously about Blaze, even when his father hadn't.

He might listen to her now.

Darcy hadn't seen Lucas since she'd heard through the grapevine that he'd moved back in with his father a few months ago. They hadn't really talked in years—not since she'd foolishly confessed her feelings for him, the night before he'd announced he'd suddenly decided to go and do his police academy training on the other side of the country. They'd kissed, and then he'd called her the next day to say he didn't actually like her that way. She didn't exactly remember how the conversation had gone. But she knew she'd yelled at him. Maybe insulted him? She wasn't sure. She'd been so heartbroken that the whole thing had been a total blur.

But her own awkwardness and embarrassment didn't matter right now. Saving lives did.

She asked her car's hands-free system to look up and dial the number for Task Force. The call was answered before it even rang once.

"Cold Case Task Force." The voice was female, professional and friendly. "This is Gemma Locke, citizen liaison. How can I help you?"

Darcy swallowed her own heartbeat and steadied her voice.

"Hi, this is Darcy Lane of the 911 North Region Dispatch Center. Is Lucas Harper there?"

"No, I'm sorry," Gemma said. "He's left for the day. Is there something I can help you with?"

"Please tell Officer Harper that I was calling for advice in relation to a concerning 911 call that came in during my shift today," she said.

Keep it professional. This was a professional call, after all. Not a personal one. The farmhouses and buildings on the edge of Sunset began to appear ahead of her. Then she spotted the large redbrick building that housed the local fire department. She didn't see Ed Harper's truck parked in his reserved spot out front. Why had Ed been so quick to dismiss the threat as a crank call? Maybe she should take the bull by the horns and ask him herself.

"Actually," Darcy added, "you can tell him that I'm going to swing by the house and talk to Ed."

After all, if she could summon enough courage to talk to Lucas after all these years, she was sure she could muster a bit more and ask Ed directly. Simon wouldn't be happy if he found out… She knew her boss wanted her to drop it. But she simply couldn't do that.

She gave Gemma her personal cell phone number, ended the call and then turned her car down the narrow country lane that led to the rustic bungalow where Ed's wife, Marie, had told her Ed was now living. Growing up, Lucas had lived with his father and stepmother in a large two-story farmhouse on the sprawling property next door. But a few months back, Ed had moved out. Lucas's stepmother had left shortly after, gone out West to live with her sister, and told Darcy to forward any packages for Ed to a different house about half a mile from the firehouse. The lane was longer, rougher and more isolated than Darcy had expected. The bungalow itself looked about a hundred years old, with a number of mismatched additions as well as sheds and garages that seemed to have randomly sprouted up around it.

Why would Lucas and Ed choose to live here instead of the beautiful farmhouse that was now sitting empty?

Ed's truck was in the driveway, and lights shone within. Darcy parked her blue vehicle in front of the garage. Red caution tape hung across the front porch, along with a sign telling her it was in need of repair and politely requesting that she head around the back. The sun began to set as she made her way around to the back of the house. Her feet crunched on the soft gravel. The wind stirred the trees around her.

Then suddenly, she heard something rustle nearby. A hand grabbed her neck roughly from behind. A cry tore from Darcy's lips, and she glanced back and saw nothing but a face shrouded in a dark gray hoodie.

"Why, Darcy Lane," Blaze's voice filled her ear. A thick, damp cloth was clamped over her mouth, stifling her ability to breathe. "I didn't expect you to involve yourself in my game. This is going to make things interesting. Now all we need is Lucas."

A thick and sickly sweet scent swamped Darcy's senses. Dizziness overwhelmed her body. Then the world went black.

"I don't know how else to put this," Lucas said, bluntly, "but there is something seriously wrong with my dad." His hands tightened on the steering wheel of his K-9 SUV. Then he glanced sideways to where his boss, Inspector Ethan Finnick, head of the Cold Case Task Force, sat in his passenger seat. "I can't thank you enough for agreeing to come for dinner and giving me your two cents on how he strikes you. Whatever's going on with him, he won't talk to me about it. He always says, 'Now is not the time for this!' But maybe he'll be different with you there."

Then again, another one of Dad's favorite sayings was "Harper men don't air their dirty laundry in public."

To say Ed had always been hard on him was putting it mildly. While he presented a charming face to the world, behind closed doors he'd always been the kind of father who was quick to point out what Lucas did wrong and incredibly slow to admit he'd done anything right.

"No problem," Finnick said. "Sometimes a second set of eyes on a situation makes all the difference in the world. Besides, Casey and Joey are going to be up on Manitoulin Island visiting family for the rest of the week." Finnick smiled when he mentioned his fiancée and son, and Lucas couldn't be happier for him. "I could use a hot meal that didn't arrive in a cardboard delivery box."

Gray-haired and in his late forties, Finnick and his cadaver K-9, Nippy, had been legends in the law enforcement community before word got out he was forming Canada's first ever Cold Case Task Force six months ago. Lucas had called Finnick up and applied to join his team the next day. Turned out, he was the only one to join the small close-knit team whom Finnick hadn't hand-selected and worked with before.

"Well, I really appreciate it," Lucas said. "He's only fifty-nine. People are talking about him maybe running for mayor when he retires as fire chief in less than a year, not that he has any interest in doing that. All I know is that in the past nine months, he's been in two minor car accidents, left my stepmother and moved out of our beautiful family home into the rundown bungalow he inherited when his brother died. And I have no idea why."

Ed had always been cranky. But Lucas had never known him to be erratic.

Could his dad have a substance abuse problem?

Was Ed having an affair?

Or had he been caught up in some kind of blackmail, crime or corruption?

Help me, God. Even guessing what it could be makes my chest hurt. My dad is hurting, and I feel helpless to assist him.

The exit for Sunset loomed ahead. Thankfully, the Ontario Cold Case Task Force had its headquarters on the northern edge of Toronto, about half an hour away. Joining the task force had given Lucas and his golden Labrador K-9, Michigan, the opportunity to come home, move back in with Ed and see what they could do to help with whatever was bothering him. Lucas glanced in the rearview mirror and caught sight of Michigan curled up in the back seat beside Nippy. Lucas's perpetually cheerful partner seemed happier than usual today due to having his new friend along with him for the ride.

Finnick nodded but didn't answer.

"Heads up, he's been living like a pack rat," Lucas went on. "He snaps at me if I try to tidy up. It's like he's afraid of losing something, but I don't know what." While Lucas had left most of his stuff at the family home—along with many of Ed's possessions—he'd been staying in the less-than-comfortable old bungalow with his dad for the time being.

He couldn't account for Ed's strange behavior. Marie had tried and failed to get a copy of his dad's medical records from the hospital. They didn't have access without his dad's legal permission—even though they were family. His whole life, Ed had been up on a pedestal, much higher than Lucas had ever had any hope of reaching himself. "I've talked to a few of his coworkers. I get the impression that he's slipping some there too, but that they're covering for him. He's been involved in fewer meetings and passing a lot of his responsibilities onto others, but that could be because he's getting closer to retirement."

"Or that he's managing to hide whatever is going on with him at work much better than he's hiding it at home," Finnick suggested.

"I don't know." Lucas shrugged. "Possibly."

"But you can tell that something's wrong and he won't open up to you about it," Finnick said.

"Exactly."

Lucas's phone began to ring from its position on the dashboard. He glanced at the screen. Gemma, the task force's resident civilian and private eye, was calling.

His K-9 partner woofed from the back seat, as if telling him to answer it.

"Pretty sure it's for me, Michi, not you," Lucas said.

"Hey!" Lucas answered the call as he merged into the right-hand lane. "You're on speaker phone. I'm in my vehicle with Finnick and the dogs. What's up?"

"Hey, guys," Gemma's voice came down the line. "Sorry to bother you after hours, but a woman named Darcy Lane, with 911 North Region, called looking for you about an emergency call that came in today. I thought you'd want to know sooner rather than later."

A warning shiver brushed his spine. Darcy Lane. He and Darcy hadn't spoken in years. She'd been his next-door neighbor growing up, the one person who'd ever looked at him like he was invincible, and the one whose heart he'd broken a few hours after their first kiss, when he'd realized that he'd only end up letting her down. Suddenly, Darcy's heart-shaped face filled his mind, with her luminous brown eyes and wisps of blond hair curling around her cheeks. She'd been beautiful, funny, tenacious, smart and more than he ever imagined he'd deserve in a best friend or girlfriend.

And he couldn't let himself get distracted thinking about her now.

What kind of emergency would she call him about?

"Thank you," Lucas said. "Did she say what it was about?"

"No," Gemma replied. "But she did say she's going to talk to your dad."

Because Lucas had been living in the bungalow in town, he'd managed to avoid running into Darcy. Which was a good thing, since when they'd last spoke, she told him that she never wanted to see him again.

It looked like he was going to come face-to-face with her sooner than expected.

"I checked the police wires," Gemma went on, "and the only odd thing I can find in your area is a false arson alarm at Meadowvale High school."

Which was chilling, considering that one of Darcy's classmates had turned out to be a very dangerous arsonist, back when he and Darcy had been students there. Lucas thanked Gemma for the call, then blew out a breath.

"Any idea what that was about?" Finnick asked after giving Lucas a moment.

"I don't know, but I don't like it," Lucas said. "I can't imagine she'd call unless it was a genuine emergency."

Instinctively, he pressed heavier on the accelerator, and he had to catch himself before he started speeding. He steered down Ed's long rural driveway and heard the rumble of a warning growl begin to form in the back of Michigan's throat. He glanced in the rearview mirror again. His partner was now sitting up straight and sniffing the air. Lucas rolled the window down, and Michigan woofed. She was alerting to the scent of a fire. Now the chill that had brushed Lucas's spine grew even colder, until it felt like a stabbing spear of ice. "Michi says we're heading into danger."

Finnick's smile had faded, and worry lines etched his brow. Finnick had been training K-9 dogs since Lucas was in kindergarten, and he knew to take a dog's alert seriously. Then Lucas felt the sting of acrid smoke reach his own nose and throat. The house came into view. Dark smoke seeped out from under his father's front door.

Lucas instructed his hands-free system to dial 911 and immediately called for firefighters and paramedics.

"One possible civilian inside," Lucas told the dispatcher. "Male, late fifties." Then he saw a bright blue car—which he was certain, at a glance, had to be Darcy's—sitting in the driveway. Lucas slammed his SUV to a stop so sharply that it shuddered. "Make that two civilians."

"I'll take over with dispatch," Finnick said. "You just go!"

Lucas leaped out and called to Michigan. The yellow Lab jumped into the front seat and bounded out after him. He ran toward the house, sensing his partner one step behind him. He burst through the caution tape that he himself had placed over the front porch, careful to avoid the boards he knew were rotting, and threw his shoulder into the front door. It popped off the rusted hinges. The air was thick with smoke, but he couldn't see flames.

"Dad!" he shouted. "Darcy!" But there was no answer except the crackle of fire eating away at the bungalow. He glanced down at his partner. Michigan wasn't specifically trained in search and rescue, but she adored Ed. "Michi! Find Dad!"

Michigan barked sharply and ran deeper into the house. Lucas followed her into the living room, pulling his sweatshirt up over his mouth and nose to block out the smoke, and praying with every step. The golden Lab dashed into the kitchen and barked so urgently she almost howled. Then Lucas heard the sound of groaning. Ed was lying on his side on the kitchen floor. Michigan nuzzled his face.

"Dad!" Lucas crouched on the ground beside him. "Are you hurt? What happened?"

"I'm fine," Ed spluttered. "I just slipped and fell. It's nothing."

Lucas didn't believe a single word of that. Blood matted the gray hair at the back of his father's head. More blood smeared the corner of the kitchen table. The tap was still running and a glass was smashed in pieces on the floor, as if Ed had been in the process of getting himself a drink when he'd been struck or pushed and fell into the table.

"Dad, it looks like you've been attacked." Lucas took his arm and helped him to his feet. "Who did this to you? Are they still here?"

His dad didn't answer.

"Where's Darcy?" Lucas asked, urgently. "Is she here? Is she okay?"

"There's no one else here." Confusion filled his father's face, only to be quickly replaced by a flash of anger. Ed yanked away from Lucas's touch, stumbled back and almost fell. "Are you deaf? Nobody attacked me. I just fell. Why are you making a big deal out of nothing?"

Help me, Lord! His mind doesn't seem right, and I don't know where Darcy is!

"I've got him," Finnick called. "You go find Darcy!"

In an instant, Finnick and Nippy had reached them. Finnick hoisted Ed up over his shoulder in a fireman's carry and ran for the exit. Nippy flanked them protectively. The faint sound of sirens rose in the air.

"I can walk, you stupid buffoon," Ed snapped at Finnick.

Finnick murmured calmly in agreement but didn't put him down.

Lucas yanked a blanket from a nearby chair, stuck it under the running tap and then left it there to get drenched as he pressed deeper into the house with Michigan by his side. Thick smoke billowed down the hallway toward him.

"Darcy!" he shouted. "Darcy, can you hear me?"

The basement door was open. A wall of bright orange flame engulfed the staircase, reducing the steps to ash before his eyes.

"Lucas!" Darcy's screams rose from beyond the flames. "Help me!"

TWO

Burning air seared Darcy's lungs as if disintegrating the very words on her tongue. She'd woken up, propped up in a wooden chair in a basement, with her ankles and wrists tied to its arms and legs, and a taste like burnt sugar in her mouth. The fog of confusion swamped her brain. Panicked prayers filled her heart. To her right, the stairs were ablaze in flames so bright they stung her eyes. Her only exit was through the fire. She was trapped, with no way out. "Help!" she screamed again.

How did she get here? Had she been drugged? Was she even still at Ed's?

She wasn't sure if she'd really heard Lucas calling her name or if the drugs and smoke were playing tricks with her mind. She could feel the pull of unconsciousness dragging at the edges of her mind, tempting her to give in and pass out again. Darcy rocked back and forth in her chair, thrashing against her bonds.

She was not about to let herself die down here.

"Lucas!" she screamed as loudly as she could, but this time her voice was barely more than a pitiful and pain-filled cry.

Save me, Lord!

She rocked harder, slamming the legs of the chair against

the floor, hoping to break herself free. A chair leg caught on the carpet. She toppled over sideways and her head smashed against the floor. The wooden chair cracked and splintered. She kicked her legs, breaking the chair even further, and fought the bonds holding her wrists until she could pull her right hand free. But already she could feel her body growing weaker. The smoke stung her eyes and was now so thick she could barely see. With a groan, the stairs collapsed completely, caving in with a thunderous crash and leaving nothing but a pile of flaming wood and debris. Tears ran down her cheeks.

Help me, God. I'm not going to make it.

"Hold on, Darcy!" Lucas's strong voice reached her through the panic and flames. "I'm coming!"

A dog barked and Darcy opened her eyes to see a flash of golden fur leaping toward her through the flames. She gasped and pulled herself up onto her hands and knees as the beautiful dog rushed toward her. The Lab reached her side, nuzzled her snout under Darcy's face and licked her cheek as if urging her to stay awake. The dog's fur was wet, and a sob slipped from Darcy's lips as she wrapped her arms around the animal as best she could. Then she looked up to see Lucas jumping down through the open doorway into the flames to save her, with what looked like a giant cape wrapped around his shoulders. He ran toward her and breathed a prayer of thanksgiving when his eyes met hers. He draped the sopping-wet blanket over her and the dog, then ducked underneath it like they were kids hiding in a damp blanket fort.

"Darcy! Are you okay?" His hands cradled the sides of her face and in an instant, it was like the past eight years had just been stripped away, along with all the awkwardness and silence there'd been between them. Lucas was here. Her best friend was back. He'd always been her hero, and now he was here to rescue her.

Everything was going to be okay.

"Lucas." She breathed his name like a sigh as relief filled her core. He'd grown up and filled out. But his green eyes and the way his brown hair fell were just like she remembered. "I'm okay, I think. But I'm kind of tied to this chair. Am I still at Ed's? Have you seen him?"

"Yes, and he made it out." Worry filled his green eyes. He looked uncertain. Unsteady, even. And already she could feel that sense of reassurance she'd just wrapped around herself begin to slip. "What happened? Who did this to you?"

"I'm not exactly sure," she said. Memories floated, disjointed and fragmented, through her mind. "Someone in a hoodie. His voice was distorted, and I didn't see his face. I think he chloroformed me or something, and I woke up here. It's all kind of a blur. But *you* know what's going on, right?"

It was a rhetorical question. She instinctively expected him to say yes.

"No," Lucas said. "But right now, all that matters is getting you out of here."

She felt his fingers slide down her wrists, then heard the clink of a pocketknife opening. In an instant, he'd cut what remained of her bonds from her wrists and ankles. Then his strong arm slid around her waist. He held her tightly to his side.

"Come on," he said. "We're going to have to break a window."

He led her through the darkness across the basement floor, still covered under the limited protection of the wet blanket. She could feel the dog nestled there behind them, its gentle snout prodding the back of her legs as they walked, as if reassuring Darcy. Together they pushed into the laundry room, where they stopped at the washer and dryer.

"One second," Lucas said. He slipped out from under the blanket and jumped up onto the washing machine. Then she heard the sounds of smashing glass and Lucas shouting to someone for help. A second later, he leaped back down to her side. "I'm going to lift you up and you're going to climb through the window, okay?"

Before she could answer, his strong hands grabbed ahold of her waist and lifted her up into the air. The blanket fell from her shoulders as she climbed up onto the washing machine. The sound of wood crashing down boomed from somewhere behind them. The floor above was beginning to cave in. But she could feel fresh, clean air rushing in from the open basement window. Emergency lights flickered in the distance as help rushed down the road toward them. Lucas's hands slid down to her feet, supporting her weight as she scrambled up. "Don't look back. I'll be right behind you."

As she crawled through the window, she found a second man, with gray hair and a black Labrador retriever, waiting for her. He grabbed ahold of her wrists and helped pull her through the narrow window. Darcy crawled out onto the grass.

"I'm Inspector Ethan Finnick, head of the Cold Case Task Force." The man helped her to his feet and led her away from the burning house, which firefighters, law enforcement and paramedics were beginning to gather around. "Call me Finnick. Everybody does. And this here is Nippy, short for Nipissing." The dog nuzzled her hand. Darcy had the impression this was the seasoned officer's attempt at helping keep her calm and grounded. "Are you okay? Are you hurt?"

"I'm okay," she said. "Just shaken."

"Did you see anyone else in the home?"

"No. Just Lucas."

Darcy tried to clear her lungs. But her breaths came quick and shallow, and she was unable to fully fill her core with oxygen. Her mind still felt as hazy as the thick smoke that had swirled around her in the basement, keeping her from thinking straight.

Finnick's brows drew together. "We should move away from the house while we—"

"I'm not going anywhere without Lucas," she cut him off, before he could even finish the thought.

She was pretty certain that Finnick wanted to rush her farther away from the house. It was probably even protocol. But she'd dig her heels in until she saw Lucas make it out safely.

Despite their complicated past, he had still once been her best friend in the world, he'd just saved her life and she couldn't turn away until she knew he was okay. Her eyes locked on the empty basement window, willing Lucas to appear. The golden Lab wriggled out and dashed across the grass toward the black Lab. The two dogs greeted each other seriously, with their heads bowed and tails wagging, as if both needed to double-check the other was all right.

Then Darcy saw Lucas's face appear through the open window, and she had to steel herself to keep from running to him. Instead, she waited, her heart pounding in her chest, as Lucas crawled through the open window, stumbled to his feet and jogged toward them.

Soot streaked the handsome lines of his face. His dark eyes fixed on her. Without even thinking, she reached for him and Lucas enveloped her in a hug. Out of the corner of her eyes, she was half-aware of Finnick signaling Nippy to his side, and then the K-9 team was running toward the first responders, leaving her and Lucas behind. For a long moment, Darcy and Lucas just stood there, holding each other tightly.

Then, slowly, Lucas pulled away and she did too. With the end of the hug came an uncomfortable tension, as if both were waiting for the other one to be the first to leap into the awkward conversation they knew they needed to have.

There were so many things she'd told herself that she'd say to Lucas Harper if she ever saw him again. She'd planned to demand an explanation about why he'd kissed her if he hadn't really liked her that way, and how he could've ended their friendship. She'd mentally rehearsed giving him a piece of her mind and letting him know just how upset he'd made her.

She'd definitely been going to ask him for an apology.

But that was a long time ago. They'd been kids then... She didn't know him anymore. Despite that she'd been so happy to see him moments ago, so grateful for his rescue, it hit her that the man before her was a stranger. If she brought up the past now, would Lucas just disappear on her again? The last time they'd gotten close he'd suddenly fled from her across the country and vanished from her life. She couldn't risk that happening again.

The important thing right now was having Lucas on her side. Fortunately, she'd gotten pretty good at shelving her uncomfortable thoughts and inconvenient feelings in her job as a 911 dispatcher. She could do it again

"I'm sorry about the house," she said.

"It's okay," he said. "It didn't really have anything of value inside it. The only thing that really mattered was getting you and Dad out safely." His voice hitched slightly, and she heard him swallow hard. "Which we did."

Darcy sucked in a deep breath and, for the first time since escaping the building, felt fresh, clean air fully fill her lungs. *Thank You, God, for that.* The yellow Lab pushed in between them, and Lucas ran his hand over the dog's head.

"Good dog, Michi," he said.

"Mishy?" Darcy asked.

"Short for Michigan," Lucas said. "Ontario RCMP K-9s are named after bodies of water."

"Which would explain Nipissing," she said.

"How are you feeling?" Lucas reached out but stopped himself from actually touching her.

"Okay," she said, stepping back slightly. "A bit foggy and confused. My mind is still really blurry."

"It's okay," Lucas said. "Just be patient. Keep taking deep breaths and it'll clear."

But she didn't want to be patient. It felt incredibly urgent that she remember everything right now—even if she didn't know why.

She looked over to see Finnick and Nippy jogging back toward them.

"I've told the authorities that as far as we know, there's no one left in the house," Finnick called. "Lucas, your dad has already left in an ambulance. One arrived pretty much immediately after I got him outside, even before the fire trucks. The paramedics insisted on taking him to the hospital for that gash on the back of his head. He took a pretty hard blow."

"And I'm guessing he insisted he was fine," Lucas said and frowned. "Darcy thinks she was chloroformed, so it's possible dad was too. He might not even remember it, and I doubt there'd be any trace of it left in his body. Do you know which hospital they took him to?"

"They didn't know," Finnick said as he reached them. "They said it depended on who could take him right away."

"I'm his emergency contact, so I'll be called when he's booked in somewhere," Lucas said. "At least for now, I know he's safe and in good hands."

Bright orange flames still billowed from the bungalow, clashing in the air with powerful sprays of water from the firefighter's hoses as they began to battle the blaze. Together Lucas, Darcy, Finnick and the dogs walked farther away, to the edge of a neighboring field. Police and paramedics were still pouring into the driveway.

"How did they get here so fast?" Darcy asked.

"Michigan detected the fire," Lucas said, "so we were able to call it in even before we got here. His specialty is arson."

Interesting choice, Darcy thought.

She turned to Finnick. "What's his specialty?"

"Cadavers," he said.

Darcy silently thanked God that Nippy's specialty hadn't been needed today.

"I feel like we should do something to help fight the fire," Darcy said.

"I get the urge," Lucas said, "especially as I've done my share of volunteering with the fire department. But the local fire department is a tight and professional team, and the last thing they need is us getting in the way as they do their job."

He was right and she knew it. It was the same with her role as a 911 dispatcher. But somehow it was ten times harder to stand by and let other first responders do their job when she was there in person instead of on the other side of the screen.

"Besides," Lucas added, and something softened in his voice, "I think the most important thing that Finnick, the pups and I can do right now is make sure you're safe. What do you remember? Gemma said you were upset about a 911 call?" he prompted, and pieces of what happened that day floated back to her. "Then you came here to talk to Ed about it and got attacked?"

"It was Blaze," she said, suddenly. As unbelievable as the statement was, the words flew from her lips, and something inside her was absolutely certain that they were true. Lucas stopped walking so sharply she almost walked into him. "Well, a Blaze copycat. He called 911 and threatened to burn down the school." She remembered the voice now, the chilling threat.

Lucas turned toward her, and she watched as his face paled. His mouth opened, then shut again.

"Who's Blaze?" Finnick asked, apparently before Lucas could find his voice.

"A really dangerous arsonist," Lucas said, turning to the older officer, "who's been dead for about eight years. Blaze was a moniker. His real name was Robby Lamb. Darcy figured out that the arsonist wreaking havoc in Sunset was him, and my dad got him to confess." He turned back to Darcy. "Are you absolutely sure it was Blaze?"

"Pretty sure," Darcy said. "Obviously not Robby Lamb, but a new version of Blaze, using the same disguise and voice."

"Is it possible that you're misremembering Blaze being involved?" Lucas asked, gently. "I mean, the fact you were drugged and caught in a fire could impact your memory."

"No!" she said, her voice rising sharply; then she took a deep breath. "I'm sorry. The whole Blaze thing happened before the fire. If I remember correctly, I even mentioned him on the dispatch call."

Slowly, she ran through the phone call, as best as she could remember, while the rest of the memories began to fall into place. Then she told them about being attacked outside the house and regaining consciousness in the basement.

"Blaze said something about not expecting me to get involved in his game," Darcy said. "But I can't remember exactly what he said. I still have some memory gaps and things I'm unclear about."

"That could be the drugs," Lucas said, "the trauma of the attack, the fire or some combination of all the above. You'll remember what you need to. I'm certain it'll come to you, along with any other important details you missed. Also, I'm sure the call has been forwarded to police."

"And there was no fire at the high school, right?" Finnick asked. "Gemma told us that was a false alarm?"

"Yeah," Darcy said. "Which is really confusing. Because I was convinced this new Blaze guy was threatening the school, and I have no idea why Ed's bungalow was set on fire." She ran both hands through her hair. "But now they're going to know the threat was real, the call wasn't a hoax, and they'll cancel the press release. Right? Even if I was wrong about the target. After all, the Blaze copycat could still be planning on setting fire to the school."

She turned to Lucas, expecting to see reassurance in his face. But instead, doubt filled his gaze.

"Hopefully," Lucas said. "But Ed said he didn't see anyone here, and it'll be up to the local fire marshal to investigate how the fire started. Considering the state the place was in, they might not be able to determine if it was arson." Not the response she'd been expecting.

"I'm sending Gemma a quick text asking her if she can find out if that press release has been sent out yet," Finnick said, glancing down at his phone. Barely seconds later, they heard Finnick's phone ping. "Yeah, it's out and Gemma's already got it off the wires. As far as everyone knows, the 911 call that led to the high school being evacuated was a false alarm."

"So we have to get Ed to tell the fire department to put out a new press release warning that people might still be in danger," Darcy said and turned to Lucas. "Obviously, as long as Ed thinks the Blaze call was a hoax, nobody's going to take the threat seriously." But the threat *was* serious—Blaze had just tried to kill her and Ed. Others were in danger too.

After all, the first threat he'd made suggested he wouldn't hesitate to target kids. He was a danger to Sunset.

"I hear you, but we might not be able to talk Dad into doing that," Lucas said. Red and blue shadows danced down the strong lines of his jaw as more police cruisers pulled up. "Fact of the matter is, there was no fire at the school, the caller didn't threaten Ed's house and you're the only one who saw this Blaze copycat. Dad can be pretty insistent and stubborn when he's made his mind up. Even if investigators do determine it could be arson, it might take a few days and it might not be conclusive. We don't want to create mass panic across town. That might be playing straight into this new Blaze's hands."

"What?" Darcy couldn't believe what she was hearing. When she'd first called Lucas for help, she'd been so certain that he was the one person who'd be able to see what was going on. "Isn't it better to create panic than risk people's lives? You need to go talk to your dad and convince him to tell everyone that he was wrong and Sunset is in danger."

Lucas didn't seem convinced.

"I'll try my best," Lucas said, "but I don't know if I can. I don't have time to go into it right now, but we can't count on Dad to do anything right now."

"I'm not counting on him," she said. "I'm counting on you!" The words flew from her lips before she realized what she was saying. The taste of sweetness and ash still lingered on her tongue, and she could feel the sting of the smoke in her throat. "People might die if Ed doesn't admit he was wrong, and you're the only one who can make him do that!"

"I know," Lucas's voice rose to match hers. "Believe me, I get it. But this is all brand-new information to me. I'm just finding out about this now and I'm still playing catch-up, and obviously my dad's on the way to the hospital." His mind reeled with all that had happened. He'd nearly lost his dad and Darcy. Now an enemy from their past might be back. He needed to think.

"But you believe me?" Darcy pressed. The conviction in her eyes reminded him of when they were teens.

"Of course I believe you," Lucas said. "At least, you're telling me the truth to the best of your memory. And I promise you that I'm going to do my very best to talk my dad into sending out a new press release."

For weeks, he'd been feeling helpless about the fact that he couldn't get a handle on what his dad was going through and didn't know how to help him. And now that feeling was crashing over his heart like a wave.

Lord, I don't exactly like knowing that I'm letting her down. But I can't instantly fix what's going on with my dad, as much as I might want to. Please, show me what to do, especially if people are in danger.

Her dark eyes filled with a look of frustration that bordered on indignation. It seemed like it hadn't even crossed her mind that Lucas might not be able to just leap into action and get his dad to stop this new threat dead in its tracks. But then again, Darcy had always had so much faith in him.

Suddenly, he remembered how he'd felt years ago, in the moments after she'd confessed her feelings for him and he'd found himself kissing her. It was like she'd put him on a pedestal, way up in the clouds, from which he'd always known that one day he was going to fall.

"Listen to me." He wished he could reach out and touch her. "I have no idea what my dad will or won't agree to do. But I promise that I take you seriously. I'm sure Finnick does, too, and we'll do everything in our power to make sure that you're safe and that this attacker is stopped before he can hurt anyone else."

For a moment, he thought Darcy was going to keep arguing. But instead she closed her eyes and whispered a prayer, and then, as he watched, calm washed over her features. Her luminous dark eyes opened again, this time filled with a steely and professional look that he'd never seen there before. He was suddenly reminded that she was no longer the teenage friend who'd relied on him for help, but a 911 dispatcher, who'd stepped up to take matters into her own hands when Ed had let her down.

"I don't think I should wait a second longer to give my statement to local police," Darcy said and stepped away.

"You sure?" Lucas said. "I get that you want to sound the alarm, but you also want to be careful not to spread misinformation if you still have memory gaps."

"Yeah," Darcy said. "I still feel a bit foggy and more than a little confused about what's going on. So I'll make it really clear about which things I'm not certain about. But people need to be warned that Blaze is back—or at least, there's somebody pretending to be him."

Then before he could even respond, she turned away from him toward the closest flashing cruiser.

"Hang on," Lucas called. "Do you want me to come with you?"

"Thanks, but I'm good." She didn't even turn.

He watched as Darcy strode toward the crowd of first responders. In an instant, he'd lost sight of her. Then Lucas felt Michigan bump her head against his hand, as if knowing that something was rattling him. Lucas reached down and ran his fingers over his partner's neck.

Had Darcy always been so stubborn and so driven? He suspected so. Slowly, he started walking in the same direction. Not exactly following her but definitely closing the distance between them. Finnick and the two K-9s matched pace.

"Should we follow her?" Lucas asked. "I'm worried her memories aren't solid yet. She could misremember something, or misinterpret something that happened, and send investigators down the wrong path or wreck her own credibility."

"I'm concerned about that too," Finnick said. "In my experience, it's dangerous for people to overestimate what they think they know. But we also can't stop her... So, what's the story between you and Darcy? I get the impression there's some history there."

He sighed. "We were next-door neighbors and best friends growing up, but we haven't really spoken in years," Lucas said, brushing aside the complicated aspects of his history with Darcy.

"I guess that I have history with pretty much every cop, firefighter, paramedic and civilian converging on this scene," Lucas added, lightly. "Sunset might be on the edge of Toronto, and a lot of our population work in the big city, but Sunset itself is a small town at heart."

"Uh-huh," Finnick said. But his boss's raised brow told Lucas that Finnick was onto him and knew he was trying to change the subject. "And I'm guessing things between you ended badly?" Finnick asked. "Considering you told me that she never wants to see you again?"

"I broke her heart," Lucas admitted, "over the phone, and she lost it with me. I never told her, or my dad, that I was rejected when I applied for the police academy in Ontario after high school. While I didn't full out lie to her, I definitely let her believe I was going to be sticking around locally. I didn't tell her when she bought me an Ontario Police College sweatshirt as a graduation gift to celebrate getting into the academy. I let her make plans for us, buy us both tickets to a concert I knew I wouldn't be going to and promised her I'd be front row at the big school play she was going to be stage manager for that fall." He sighed as the memories came back.

"The longer I went without telling her, the more embarrassed I got and the harder it became. I think I was in denial and just hoped I'd be able to reapply here before I was due to start training in B.C." But that hadn't happened, and he'd left. He continued, "She was completely blindsided when I told her that I was suddenly moving across the country. I think she took it personally—" *probably because I'd just kissed her* "—and like I was running away from her. Even though I tried to tell her it had nothing to do with her. She got really upset."

I hate you, you're a coward, and I never want to see you again, Lucas Harper!

She'd been crying too. And her words had seared themselves on his mind ever since, replaying over and over again like an unwanted record.

After all, he had been a coward. Just not in the way she'd thought.

"Do you really think she meant it?" Finnick asked, gently. "Or even remembers what she said? It was years ago, and she was hurt. Not that I'm justifying anything she might've said. But when I tried to get her to move away from the house, she seemed pretty determined that she wasn't going anywhere until you made it out safely."

Had she?

"Well, Darcy's never been the kind of person who cares about something halfway," Lucas replied. "She's always been all in or all out…"

And it was better to leave that mess in the past than risk another blowup now.

Lucas glanced toward Darcy in the crowd. The bungalow behind her was nothing but a charred pile of matchsticks, so there'd be no excuse for Ed, Lucas and Michigan not to move back into the family house now. Looked like Darcy was about to become his neighbor again. But they were pretty big properties, with a patch of forest in between. The road in and out was narrow and unpaved, but he could still get to her quickly if she needed him.

"So, it was Darcy who told your dad about Blaze... Would she feel betrayed by him now?" Finnick asked.

"Probably," Lucas said, "but I can understand law enforcement not wanting to cause undue panic. Blaze wasn't just an arsonist. He was like this twisted tormentor who seemed intent on stirring up as much fear in the community as he could. He'd post videos of himself to the internet, with his face hidden in a gray hoodie, taunting all of us with this eerie, distorted voice. Everyone was on edge, jittery and suspicious, wondering where he'd strike next."

"Larger than life?" Finnick asked.

"Very much so," Lucas said. "And my fear is that now my dad has decided this new copycat is a hoax, he'll dig his heels in, even though the house he's been living in just burned down."

Although, he had no idea why his father would do that. Clearly there was a threat out there, and they needed to deal with it.

They continued to press through the crowd at the front of the house, with Michigan and Nippy flanking them on either side. Already the firefighters had extinguished the fire, leaving nothing but a sopping and charred-out skeleton of wooden beams in its wake. Both the flames and first responders had done a quick number on the ramshackle bungalow Lucas had spent weeks trying to convince Ed to move out of.

He spotted Darcy talking to a tall officer with strawberry-blond hair and a very square jaw. Instinctively, Lucas bristled. He'd known Corporal Austin Dillon since they'd played football on opposing teams in high school. Austin was the kind of player who'd always seemed to enjoy hitting too hard, bullying weaker players and telling inappropriate jokes because he liked how they made other people uncomfortable. He'd won a lot, and that was because he'd cheated a lot.

But that was years ago, when they'd been teenagers and before they'd both become cops.

Lord, help me to keep an open mind and not judge anyone based on who they used to be.

Which was always a good reminder, even when there wasn't a potential arsonist on the loose.

"Lucas!" A female voice called his name before he could reach Darcy and Austin. He looked to see a remarkably pretty paramedic, with a pair of large glasses and a shiny black braid, jogging toward him through the crowd. It was Nicola Matthews. She was the wife of a friend he'd had since kindergarten, a stellar paramedic—and also Robby Lamb's older sister.

"Nicola!" he called back. "Do you know which hospital Dad was taken to?"

"North Toronto," she said. "I know it's not the closest one. But that's a pretty nasty cut on the back of his head, and they wanted a concussion specialist team to take a look at him. Can you explain to me what's happening?"

"No, I can't," Lucas said, and he wasn't going to speculate. He stepped back as she reached them. "Nicola, this is Finnick, head of the Ontario Cold Case Task Force. Finnick, Nicola Matthews was awarded top paramedic of the region last year. Her husband, Officer Pauly Matthews, is a local cop."

Finnick reached out to shake her hand. "It's nice to meet you."

"It's nice to meet you too." Nicola said. She returned the handshake. Then Nicola turned to Lucas. "You can imagine my shock this afternoon when I was in the ambulance, rushing a heart attack victim to the hospital, and suddenly an all-hands call comes over the radio saying a 'Blaze' copycat—" she made air quotes around the name *Blaze* "—had called in an arson attack against the school."

She huffed out a breath.

"Then I get called to a fire here," she went on, frustration rising in her voice, "and Ed tells of some 911 dispatcher who was taken in by a hoax." She shook her head. "You know the whole town is going to be talking about this by tomorrow. People are going to get paranoid and start seeing my dead brother behind every tree, and my mother is going to be emotionally devastated by having this all dragged up again."

Nicola and Robby's mom, Bea, had never believed that her son was guilty of anything. She'd plagued law enforcement, politicians and the press for years with phone calls and letters demanding her son's name be exonerated. He couldn't imagine how stressful that must be for Nicola.

"Do you know who the dispatcher was who got tricked?" Nicola asked.

Help me, Lord. I'm not about to lie to her, but I also want to keep Darcy's name out of this as long as possible.

Not that it wouldn't get out sooner or later, especially as she was currently making a statement to police.

This whole mess could spin out of control so fast, and I need Your guidance.

"I'm so sorry to hear about your brother," Finnick cut in. "I imagine his loss was pretty hard on your family."

Nicola eyed him thoughtfully for a moment. Lucas felt Michigan press up against him and ran his hand over the dog's side.

"I must say, that's not most people's response when they hear that Robby was my brother," she said, finally. "Yes, it was hard. My mom is still convinced he was innocent and killed by a fire set by the real arsonist. She goes online looking for conspiracy theories that either Robby wasn't actually Blaze and that the real Blaze killed him in that fire. She says she won't rest until Robby's name is cleared."

"Again, I'm so sorry to hear this," Finnick said before Lucas could come up with a response. Lucas noticed that he'd changed the subject from the 911 dispatcher who'd taken the call. The seasoned cop was doing a good job of deflecting. "I can't imagine how hard this must be for you, your mother and the whole family, really. What was he like?"

Nicola hesitated again, as if she'd mentally geared herself up for a fight, yet something about Finnick's calm and respectful demeanor had taken the wind out of her sails. "He cared deeply about things." Her shoulders bowed. "Maybe too deeply."

"I'm sorry too," Lucas added. He ran his hand over the back of Michigan's head and felt the dog's comforting snout nudge his fingers. He couldn't imagine how the constant smell of smoke in the air must be impacting the arson dog's well-honed senses. "I honestly wish I could explain what's going on. This whole situation's a mess to me, and I haven't spoken to my dad since we found him in the house. But if we find out something solid, I promise I'll let you know."

A male paramedic called Nicola's name from somewhere within the crowd. Far more emergency vehicles had descended than were needed, and her vehicle was now being redeployed.

"Thanks," she said, then nodded to both of them and started back toward the ambulance.

As she walked away, Lucas could see Darcy heading back toward them.

Lucas watched as Darcy gave Nicola a quick but sincere-looking hug before she passed. Then the two women parted ways, and Darcy continued toward them. Faint lines of soot still traced the beautiful lines of her face, like someone had sketched her features out of charcoal. Darcy's dark eyes looked up and met Lucas's, and he watched as worry pooled in their depths. He felt the echo of her concern rumbling inside his own heart, like thunder warning of a coming storm.

Lord, I don't have the first clue what's going on with this new Blaze copycat. All I know is somebody attacked Darcy, tied her up in the basement and tried to take her life.

Please give me the strength and wisdom I need to protect her and keep her safe.

The pain of losing her friendship for years was nothing compared to knowing she could lose her life because he was unable to stop it.

Michigan stepped away from Lucas's side and bounded over to greet Darcy as she reached them. The dog butted against Darcy's leg with her tail wagging and head bowed, as if the K-9 sensed Darcy was upset.

"Well, I reported everything that happened to Corporal Austin Dillon," Darcy said as she joined them. "He listened and took a lot of notes, but he also seemed concerned that Ed's version of events is very different from mine. I kind of felt like he was humoring me, and I don't know if he really took me seriously. He did mention he belongs to the same golf club as your dad."

"Well, hopefully he'll be able to keep an open mind," Lucas said, and sighed. "Although, we'll be pretty hard-pressed to find anyone in a thirty-mile radius who doesn't already have an opinion on Blaze, Robby Lamb's death and my dad."

"Would a fresh set of eyes help?" Finnick asked.

For the first time in longer than he could remember, Lucas felt a sudden burst of hope fill his heart.

"Yes!" Darcy exclaimed, and Lucas could hear something like hope in her voice too.

"Absolutely," Lucas said.

"On it." Finnick reached for his phone. "I'm going to call in the team."

THREE

Lucas knew that if it was up to Darcy, they'd have leaped into his SUV immediately and rushed to the Cold Case Task Force offices. Instead, they had to wait until the firefighters and first responders wrapped up the scene and Lucas placed a call to the hospital to confirm his dad was checked in and doing well. By the sound of things, they wanted to keep Ed overnight for observation, just in case his injuries were more serious than they first appeared, and while the hospital couldn't give him too many specifics, it sounded like Ed's grumpiness was giving the nurses a run for their money.

There wasn't much to be salvaged from the bungalow. Everything was gone, from Michigan's spare dog bed up to the rafters. Thankfully, he'd dropped off the bulk of his belongings at his family home and had been keeping only a rucksack's worth of stuff in the bungalow. But while it seemed to him like not much of value had been lost in the fire, he knew his dad might have a very different opinion.

Darcy drove her car back to her house, with Lucas and Finnick following behind in his K-9 SUV. Then they all drove to the task force headquarters together, with Darcy sitting in the passenger seat and Finnick insisting on being in the back with the dogs, joking that every rookie knew it was secretly the best seat in the vehicle. It was almost an hour before they finally reached the offices on the north end of Toronto. The town house had two floors of offices, plus an attic that Gemma was currently converting into a research library.

The smell of fresh paint filled the air, along with the tempting scent of a pile of pizzas that Officer Caleb Perry had picked up for them on his way in. Now Lucas, Finnick, Gemma and Caleb sat around in a circle of chairs, waiting for Darcy, who'd gone to freshen up. Nippy and Michigan stretched out on the floor in front of the heating vent, and Gemma's conure parrot, Rippi, bounced cheerfully in his cage in the corner of the room. The only member of the team who hadn't made the meeting was Gemma's brother, Sergeant Jackson Locke, who had already been halfway up to Clearwater with his K-9 partner, Hudson.

Lucas studied his boss, who appeared deep in thought. "What's up?" Lucas asked.

"Just thinking..." Finnick responded. "I recognize that name—Pauly Matthews. I actually remember Nicola's husband's application to the K-9 program, and a colleague mentioning that Pauly Matthews's late brother-in-law was a teenage arsonist." He ran his hand over the back of his neck.

Interesting... Lucas and Pauly had been kindergarten friends, but he hadn't realized.

"I remember there was an...incident...when he didn't make the cut. He was upset—made an angry parting remark about how when your wife's brother is an arsonist, it's hard to advance in law enforcement."

Lucas listened intently now. "Do you think that was actually part of it?"

Finnick shrugged, noncommittally. "In my experience, people in law enforcement come from all kinds of backgrounds," he said, "including those with difficult family connections. The K-9 unit is pretty competitive. I'm not there anymore, but he could always reapply and try again. Many people do."

Lucas nodded. Had Pauly ever reapplied? Maybe not, if he was still working for the local PD.

"Anyway, this was years ago now," Finnick said. "He emailed later and apologized for the outburst, but it was clear the issue was a sore spot."

"I've always known Pauly to be a great guy," Lucas said, "and head over heels in love with Nicola. And of course I failed the first time I applied to cop training in Ontario, too."

Finnick nodded, and understanding filled his gaze.

Then Lucas heard footsteps on the old wooden floors and looked up to see Darcy walking in. He instinctively stood, then hesitated awkwardly on his feet for a moment while Gemma invited her to help herself to pizza and Caleb showed her where the cold drinks were.

For the first time since rescuing Darcy from the darkened basement, he was able to take a really good look at her. She'd washed her face clean from soot, dirt and makeup. Her blond hair was still short, just like it had been in high school. But it was a softer cut now, with a few loose wisps brushing the sides of her face. She'd been sixteen when he'd seen her last. She was now twenty-four, about two years younger than he was. And while he could tell she'd aged since he'd seen her last, it was in a way that made her more confident and secure in herself. She'd always been cute. But now she was the kind of stunning that could make a man stare if he wasn't careful.

No, he couldn't let himself think that way.

He'd ruined any possibility of ever having that kind of relationship with her years ago when he'd broken her heart. Her pain had seemed pretty deep, and her words had definitely been scathing. He was probably the last guy she'd consider for a relationship, and the last thing he wanted right now was to risk jeopardizing the case by complicating things.

Darcy sat down, and Finnick launched into a more formal introduction to the team and its members. Darcy was sitting less than six inches away from Lucas, yet the look in her eyes was like she was a million miles away. She nibbled at her pizza, nodding at various members of the team as they were introduced, then gave up pretending she was going to eat it, set it down on the floor beside her and leaned forward on her elbows.

"Sorry, we're still in boxes and painting," Finnick said. "We planned to take possession of the building at the end of March but were delayed almost two months due to some unexpected construction and maintenance that had to be done before we could move in."

Darcy nodded. "I'm sorry if this is an odd question," she said, glancing around the room, "but why are you here instead of at one of the large regional police centers?"

"Because we're independent." Finnick leaned back and crossed his arms. "Basically, we've got two jobs. The first is solving cold cases that other law enforcement agencies failed to solve. The other is reopening old closed cases we have reason to believe were miscarriages of justice. That means I have the ability to pull people in from local, regional, provincial and federal law enforcement as needed. It also means we might end up annoying a whole lot of officers who don't like us poking around in their business." He assessed her a moment before saying, "I want you to start at the beginning and take it slow. We'll start with you and then have Lucas fill in as needed."

Both Caleb and Gemma pulled out notepads. Lucas had first met them both in December, when Gemma had invited him to join them for Christmas a couple of weeks before the team had officially launched. Caleb was RCMP and blond, with boyish good looks that Lucas had already noticed turned women's heads. The good looks were coupled with the kind of cynicism that made Lucas think he'd once been betrayed and never forgiven himself for it. Gemma was a licensed private eye, with short dark hair and the same blue eyes as her brother, Jackson. She had a habit of working overtime and digging far deeper into cases than Finnick asked her to. Lucas was thankful to have them both on his team.

Darcy started by going over the disturbing 911 call she'd received, reciting back the man's words as best as she could remember them and outlining why she thought it was a threat against the school. Her memory of the events seemed to be clearer and crisper now. It appeared whatever lingering effects the attack had on her mind were fading fast.

"Apparently the call was a false alarm," she said. "Which I'm very confused by, because everything in my gut told me it was a threat against the school. Hoax calls are dangerous. The problem with false alarms is that then people stop taking real threats seriously. Especially teenagers. Too many false alarms in a given year, they'll just start assuming all emergency evacuations are fake. They'll shuffle their feet as slowly as possible or even just hide in a bathroom or closet and wait it out."

"So, he never specifically identified himself as Blaze, but you thought it was him?" Finnick confirmed. "Or at least, a really good copycat?"

"Yeah," Darcy said. "It wasn't just the same distorted voice. It was the same tone of voice and way of talking. If I didn't know any better, I'd have suspected it was actually Blaze himself."

"You can make a computer-generated deepfake of anybody's voice with a large enough sample size," Gemma said.

"And the caller would have access to any number of videos that are still floating around online since the last spate of attacks."

Caleb leaned forward. "Do you think that the Blaze who talked to you on the phone today is the same Blaze who set fire to those buildings eight years ago?"

The question was pointed, and Darcy squirmed slightly.

"Well, obviously that's impossible," she said. "There was never any question that Robby was the one who died in that fire."

"That's not what I asked," Caleb said. "Forget about what's possible or not. Was this copycat so on point that you think he's the same guy?"

"Maybe." Darcy shrugged. "It definitely sounded like him."

"According to you," Caleb said. "But Ed, the fire chief, disagreed. And then the fire department put out a press release calling the 911 call a hoax. How do you explain that?"

Darcy met his sharp look straight on. "I can't."

"And that's not her fault," Lucas cut in. "My dad's been going through some personal issues. He moved out of our big family farmhouse into this small bungalow, he left my stepmother and he won't talk to me about either one. So, the fact he labeled the call 'a hoax' and says he saw no one in the bungalow is incredibly unhelpful, but it isn't Darcy's fault."

If anything, it feels like mine.

"You said he spoke when he attacked you," Gemma asked, gently. "What did he say? To the best of your memory."

"Something like, 'Hello, Darcy Lane. I didn't expect you to join my game,'" she said and shuddered. "It might've been 'mess with my game,' but it was something like that. Oh, and also that I was going to make things interesting."

It felt like the members of the task force sucked in a collective breath.

"He called you by name?" Lucas asked, and she nodded.

"So he knew exactly who you were," Finnick said.

"Yeah." Her voice barely rose above a whisper. "He also vaguely mentioned Lucas. I think it was, 'Now all we need is Lucas.'"

Silence fell around the group. Lucas's heart lurched. Not that he was worried for his own safety so much as thinking that someone had used his name to torment her. He felt his hand reaching across the gap between them to take Darcy's. But instead, he caught himself, just before their fingers touched, and pulled back. She didn't seem to notice.

"Maybe not all the truth there is," Darcy said, "but it's all the truth I know right now. To summarize, he talked like Blaze, used the same voice modulator and wore the same hooded sweatshirt. I expect he studied Blaze's voice to copy his cadence, although I know his original videos were scrubbed from the internet—"

"Nothing's ever really scrubbed from the internet if you know where to look," Gemma said with a determined grin.

"I've mentally been calling him Blaze," Darcy went on, "even though I know the original Blaze is Robby Lamb, who died eight years ago. As for what happened back then, I'm sure you've got access to the police files, and there was a lot of media coverage too."

Finnick leaned back and crossed his feet at the ankles. "But we'd like to hear your version."

"Well," Darcy started, "basically, when I was sixteen and Lucas was eighteen, this guy who called himself Blaze started setting fires in my hometown. The first was a restaurant, the second was a new housing development, the third was a strip mall and the fourth was a warehouse. Thankfully, only one person was killed—a security guard who was working in the warehouse."

"And who was he?" Caleb interjected.

"His name was Jim Scott," Lucas supplied. "The man was in his early sixties and had two kids and a grandchild. No known connection to the arsonist."

He glanced at Darcy and nodded at her to continue.

"Blaze seemed to really like attention," she went on. "He fashioned himself as a vigilante for justice who was taking our town back." She shuddered. "It was really kind of gross. There were all these theories that he was an escaped convict, or a serial killer, or even a firefighter."

"So nobody was thinking it was a sixteen-year-old boy?" Caleb hazarded.

"No." Darcy ran both hands through her hair for a moment and let it fall through her fingers. "Not at all. I knew Robby Lamb from school. We were in the same grade. I thought he liked acting and architecture. He'd actually given me a flyer for some zoning-law protest about a year before the Blaze thing hit, so I had no idea he was into criminal activity. I was a member of my school's STAV Club—Stage Tech, Audio and Visual. I think his sister was in it, too, but she'd just graduated. Anyway, I painted sets and designed the special effects. Robby was one of the actors. Not the best, by any means, but the kind of guy who always wanted to be in the spotlight. And I just started to have the suspicion that Robby was Blaze."

"Why?" Caleb asked. "After all, it was a pretty far-fetched theory."

"Hang on." Lucas turned to Caleb and raised a hand. "You're badgering her."

"No, I'm not," Caleb said. "But I am going to grill her. And if you didn't have a personal relationship with her, hopefully you'd do the exact same in my shoes."

"It's fine," Darcy said. She hadn't even flinched. Darcy turned to Caleb. "It wasn't just one thing. It was a whole bunch of little things. He'd have soot under his fingers, and one day he came into rehearsal smelling like gasoline, even though he was too young to drive. He said he'd accidentally splashed it on himself when he'd been working in the garage. Well, Lucas worked in his grandfather's garage every Saturday and had never splashed gas on himself. Robby had this lighter that he really loved playing with, no matter how many times teachers told him to put it away. He also had this way of doing voices when he thought no one was listening, that just reminded me of Blaze. That's the thing about being backstage on crew—people forget you're there. It's like you're invisible. So I went and just spilled everything I was thinking to Lucas."

"And I thought her theory sounded really solid," Lucas took over the story, "so I went and argued it with my dad. It was his first year as fire chief, and for whatever reason, he thought Darcy's lead was solid…" His words trailed off. That was what he'd always told himself, but who knew what his dad had really thought about the case then or now. "Or maybe he didn't think it was all that solid, but they were grasping at any straw they could find to stop what was happening. Blaze had been terrorizing Sunset for weeks at that point. Either way, Dad went and talked to Robby, and whatever he said got Robby to confess and even turn himself into police. His parents got him out on bail. That night, he set fire to an abandoned farm on a property nearby. Apparently, it flamed a lot faster than he was expecting, and he died. His remains were confirmed by both DNA and dental records, and it was ruled an accidental death."

"What a tragedy." Finnick shook his head. Nippy raised his head and whimpered slightly, as if hearing the sadness in his partner's voice. "That poor kid and his family."

"'That poor kid'?" Caleb repeated.

"Yeah," Finnick said. "He was obviously unwell and needed help. Especially if he cracked the first time an adult took the time to really talk to him. I can't even imagine what his parents were thinking. They missed the fact he needed help and let him out of their sight the night after he'd been arrested."

"Well, I'm sure they've lived to regret it," Lucas said. According to Nicola, Robby's mother still hadn't fully accepted her son's guilt. "She has been pestering politicians, law enforcement and the press for years to reopen the case and exonerate him."

"Is it possible that Bea was the person who attacked you and Ed?" Finnick asked.

"No, she's short, out of the shape and has trouble walking due to her diabetes," Darcy said. "She's a very fiery woman, but not physically strong."

And maybe Ed's firm conviction in Robby's guilt and the confession he'd gotten from the teenager was all that stood in the way of clearing her son's name.

"I have a question." Gemma raised her hand like they were back in school. "Was it ever determined why those specific locations were chosen? Was there a pattern?"

"Not that I ever knew of," Lucas said.

"And no known connection to the security guard who died?" Caleb asked.

"No," Lucas said. "Although apparently, he was a friend of one of Pauly Matthews's uncles—Pauly's now married to Robby's sister. But that's not strange or notable in a town the size of Sunset. It seems he was just in the wrong place at the wrong time."

Gemma nodded. "And how far apart were the fires? Any discernable pattern or timing there?"

"Not that I know of," Lucas said.

"I'm just thinking that there was probably a pattern in Robby's mind," Gemma said. Her eyes were on whatever she was writing. "Not that it has to be one that makes sense to anyone else. And why would a copycat call 911 and strike Ed's house today? Is there anything special about today or this month? Is it somebody's birthday? Or the anniversary of something?"

"Again, not that I know of," Lucas admitted. "Definitely not anything high school or theater related." He glanced at Darcy for confirmation. "I mean, the drive-in always does a huge event for teenagers on the May long weekend, which is in a couple of days. Dad might know better. Hopefully, he'll be happy to explain more when he's out of the hospital. There's a slim possibility they'll let him out tonight if he insists on discharging himself. But I expect they'll succeed in keeping him overnight."

A phone chimed prettily, and Darcy reached into her pocket and pulled out her cell. Then she leaped to her feet, only to have it slip from her fingers as if it had just bitten her.

"Are you okay?" Lucas stood. "What happened?"

"It's him." Her face paled. "He's texting me now."

Lucas looked down at the screen in horror to see a picture of Darcy tied unconscious to a chair in Ed's basement, followed by the words:

My game has just begun Darcy.

Get ready to burn.

BLAZE.

* * *

Darcy's heart was beating so hard in her chest the sound of it filled her ears.

Lord, please stop whoever is behind this!

She could feel her limbs begin to shake and thought she was going to collapse. But in an instant, Lucas was beside her. His strong hand brushed the small of her back, filling her with his strength and stability. The rest of the team leaped to their feet, too, but Gemma practically dove into the middle of the circle and snatched the phone up from the floor with a victorious whoop.

"Big mistake, creeper!" Gemma charged across the room toward her computer. "You send Darcy a threatening text and I'm going to use it to track you down!" She plugged the phone into a laptop and started typing furiously as a wall of text filled her screen.

"I'm pretty sure whoever is behind this used an untraceable number," Caleb called.

Gemma snorted so hard she practically blew a raspberry. "Oh, he used an untraceable phone and blocked his number. But that just means it's going to take me slightly longer to figure out who this jerk is."

Darcy could feel the blood beginning to return to her limbs, and she pulled away from Lucas. He turned to Finnick.

"So, we're officially going to be looking into this?" Lucas asked his boss.

"Absolutely," Finnick said. "Gemma, when you're done downloading what you can from Darcy's phone, I want you to install a tracking software on it that allows us to keep track of where she is at all times—in case this Blaze copy-cat makes another attempt on her life again—an alert system she can use to contact us for help in an emergency, and also software that will download and log any suspicious calls she gets. Of course, presuming that's all okay with you, Darcy?"

"Definitely good by me," Darcy said and crossed her arms.

She wasn't allowed to use her personal phone at work, but she could keep it by her. Fresh determination filled her core. She'd never been the kind of person who backed down from a fight. And now, for the first time, it was beginning to look like this fight could be won.

"Good," Finnick said. "Also, Gemma, I want you to do a full write-up on the old Blaze case and have it to everyone by tomorrow morning."

"I'll have it done tonight," Gemma called.

"Thank you." Finnick turned to Caleb. "I want you to do what you do best—turn your doubt and cynicism up to eleven and try to disapprove everything you've heard today. I want you to prove that Robby Lamb was never Blaze, that Robby never died in that fire and that if he did die in the fire, he was murdered. While you're at it, feel free to try to prove that none of the fires were actually arson, although I advise you tread very carefully when dealing with victims."

"Gotcha." Caleb nodded seriously.

"Also, I'll be briefing Jackson," Finnick said, "and directing him to work with you on this. I know you and Jackson have different styles, but you've also been friends and colleagues for a long time, and you make an unbeatable team." He chuckled wryly. "I know I wouldn't want to go against you. Basically, I want to make sure that we can prove every single point of this case, and the best way to do that is to see if there's any facts that we can eliminate. Don't take a single fact for granted."

Caleb nodded and fired off a text, which Darcy guessed was to Jackson.

Then Finnick's grin widened, and fresh determination filled his gaze.

"That's a good note for all of you," Finnick said. "Don't take anything you think you know for granted. I want you all to second-guess everything about this case—even your own memories and perceptions." He glanced at Darcy briefly as he said this. "There are always things we don't know, and the most dangerous thing we can do is just assume what we think we know about a messy situation is right. I'm going to put a formal request in for all the case files to do with the original investigation into Robby Lamb, as well as everything to do with the 911 call today, the response to it, and the attack on Ed and Darcy."

Then he turned to Darcy again and his look softened.

"Don't worry," he said. "My team might be pretty new, but they're the best, and I promise we'll get to the bottom of this and bring whoever's behind it to justice. And if local law enforcement tries to start a turf war over jurisdictions, they'll be in for a crash course in the powers of our new Cold Case Task Force. But that'll be my job to fight, and I've got pretty big shoulders."

Darcy exhaled slowly. "Thank you."

And thank You, Lord. May this whole mess get wrapped up quickly before anyone else gets hurt.

"Now, do you have any questions for me?" Finnick asked her.

"Not ones you can answer," she said.

Finnick leaned forward. "Try me."

Darcy looked up at the ceiling. Green strips of painter's tape still lined the edges just above the walls.

"Why did Blaze taunt me with a riddle about the high school when his real target was Ed's house?" she asked.

"Why taunt me outside the house and then leave me tied up in the basement? Why text my phone now?"

"I don't know," Finnick said. "But my guess is that he wants to scare you."

"Again, there'll be a pattern," Gemma chimed in, "some reason for his action that we can't see yet."

"And what do I do?" Lucas asked.

"You're our guy on the ground." Finnick faced him. "Talk to people, chase down leads and keep us posted. You have the home-court advantage on this one. We're going to check in twice a day as a team on this, and you can pass on to Caleb and Jackson anyone you'd rather they interview or leads you want them to chase. And of course, keep Darcy and your dad safe too. I know this is asking a lot, but it sure would help us if you could get Ed to help us on the case, tell us why he didn't think the call sounded like Blaze and why it didn't match his memories of Robby."

Lucas nodded grimly. "I'll do my best. Let's all just pray that my dad finally decides to open up and talk to me."

"I still don't get it." Caleb leaned back in his chair and crossed his arms. "Why would the fire chief stand in the way of solving this case?"

"I honestly don't know," Lucas said, shrugging. "But now he's going to have no choice but to move back into our family home. Thankfully, that means Darcy and I will be neighbors again, and I'll be able to keep an eye on her and make sure she's safe."

Lucas's words were still running circles around Darcy's mind a little while later as they drove home. Finnick had taken his own vehicle back to his place, which left her alone with Lucas for the first time since he'd come back into her life. She rolled her window down a crack and let the fresh

May air flow freely through the vehicle. Suddenly, the space felt too confined with him sitting right next to her.

He glanced in her direction but didn't comment as she took a few deep breaths. For the first time in hours, her head finally felt completely clear. And somehow, the sharper and more focused her mind grew, the less things made sense.

When she'd been trapped in the basement and scared for her life, with her head swimming from drugs, smoke and fear, everything inside her had wanted to see Lucas as her rescuer and hero.

She'd wanted to forget the past and believe she could ignore it.

But the truth of the matter was, he'd had months to check in with her since returning to town. Her phone number hadn't changed, and she'd been living alone in the same home her family had always lived in after her parents had retired to Florida. He hadn't reached out to her once. Not to mention, he'd had countless opportunities to call her, text her or email her in the years since they'd last spoken. Yet now, Lucas was about to move back in next door and protect her from this new Blaze copycat?

The truth of the matter was that he'd found her in the basement because that was the house he was living in—not because he'd come looking for her. And now he was stepping up to help her because he was a good man and a cop, not because he'd suddenly decided he wanted her in his life.

Darcy's friendship with Lucas had effectively ended that single moment in that wooden gazebo on the shores of Lake Simcoe, when she'd foolishly blurted out her feelings for him and they'd kissed. Now he was only back in her life because he felt like he had to be—not because he wanted to be—and she would do good to remember that.

She glanced at him again, studying his profile in the dim

space. She could rely on him as an officer, but she couldn't rely on him for anything more.

Lord, help me to remember to put my faith in You and what You are calling me to do, instead of leaning on a man who might just let me down again.

He pulled to a stop in her driveway and got out with Michigan. They all met up together on the front step. She unlocked the door, and then she, Lucas and Michigan searched the house together for any signs of a break-in or intruder. Nothing was out of place, from the boxes of leftovers from her favorite local fusion restaurant she'd left in the fridge to the hamper of clean clothes she'd forgotten to fold at the side of her bed.

She walked Lucas and Michigan to the door.

Then she stood with him on the porch for a long moment, hesitating to say good-night but also not really having any excuse not to. Michigan pressed her head against Darcy's leg. She ran her hand over the dog's silky fur.

"Now remember, Gemma put an alert app on your phone," Lucas said. He looked down at her hand as she brushed her fingers over his K-9 partner's ears. "If anything happens or you need help, you just push it and we'll come running. I'll probably be faster on foot. I figure I can probably be there in eight to ten."

"Thank you," she said, feeling like it was the millionth time she'd said it so far today but not knowing what else to say. "I really like your team, by the way. After the call came in, I felt like nobody was taking me seriously. But your team really listened—even if a couple of them grilled me a bit. And I finally feel like somebody is actually going to do something to catch the Blaze copycat."

"Do you think it's possible that he isn't a copycat?" Lucas asked. She looked up, and his sincere green eyes met hers in the soft glow of her front porch light. "That maybe we were wrong about Robby, my dad talked an innocent kid into confessing…"

His words trailed off.

"And that the real Blaze killed Robby to cover up his crimes because of us?" Darcy heard her own voice shake as she finished the thought for him. "No, I've never thought that, and I still can't."

"Neither can I," Lucas said. "But as a member of the Cold Case Task Force, I need to keep an open mind in order to do my job."

Yeah, that was fair.

"Do you have work tomorrow?" he asked.

"Yup, but not until after lunch," Darcy said. "I'm on the afternoon shift."

"And how are you feeling about the situation?" He took a step toward her, and she could feel the space between them shrink.

"Frightened," she admitted. Then her chin rose. "But that's what he wants, right? He wants me to be frightened, and that makes me angry. It makes me determined to fight this guy, anyway I can."

"I don't think you can stop yourself from being frightened," Lucas said. His hands brushed lightly against her shoulders. "And definitely don't blame yourself for it. Just don't let the fear win."

"I won't." Her voice dropped to a whisper.

"I know," he said. "It's one of the things I like about you. You've always been one of the most stubborn and driven people I've ever met."

Lucas hesitated, his hands still touching her shoulders. Then his fingers began to slip down her arms as if he was about to take her hands, but instead he stepped back and stuffed his hands in his pockets.

"I'm not really sure how to bring this up," he added, "but I really do feel bad about what happened in the past. I'm really uncomfortable about the whole thing, and I hope you can just pretend the whole mess never happened. Unless you think we should talk about it?"

"Nah, I'm good," she said, quickly, edging away from him. "That doesn't matter right now. We don't need to dig up all that." Last thing she needed was the embarrassment of rehashing the past, let alone for him to feel like he had to explain why he hadn't liked her the way she'd liked him. "We were kids. The past is in the past. You're now a cop, and I'm a 911 dispatcher, and we're both caught up in the case."

"Right."

"Yeah."

He nodded, so did she, and for a long moment they just nodded at each other without actually saying anything.

Then he ran his hand over the back of his neck.

"Well, I'll be right next door at the old house," he said, "if you need anything."

"I guess we're going to be neighbors again."

"Yeah," he said. "I guess so."

She wanted a hug and to hear him promise yet again that he and his team would keep her safe from harm. But as he stood there, on the very same front porch they'd stood together hundreds of times before, all she could think of was how embarrassing it would be for them both if she tried to hug him when he might not want to hug her back.

So instead, she wished both Lucas and Michigan goodnight. They waited on her front porch as she closed and locked the door. Then, finally, she watched through the front window as they got back into their SUV and left. Only then did she try to eat a few leftovers, change into sweatpants and a T-shirt, and attempt to go to bed.

It was an unseasonably warm night. May was always the oddest month in Southern Ontario, fluctuating between spring and summer weather in the blink of an eye. Darcy left her bedroom window open a crack and then lay down, listening to the spring breeze brushing the trees outside. Although her body ached with the need to sleep, her mind wouldn't let her rest.

Lord, I don't know how I feel right now or even how to pray. Please heal Ed and keep him safe. Please protect me and everyone from whoever's threatening us.

Her heart ached like it was a little ball attached to a paddle with a rubber band, which kept getting smacked around wildly in every direction. It was hard to believe so much had happened in one day. Almost impossible to think it had happened in just a few hours. She'd been terrified by the phone call from Blaze, worried for the teenagers she'd thought he was after, then unbelievably confused when the call to the school had turned out to be a false alarm. That had been nothing compared to the fear that filled her mind when she was attacked and had woken up in Ed's basement.

But Lucas and Michigan had been there.

And, Lord, as thankful as I am that Lucas was there and that his team is there for me, I'm embarrassed to admit that part of me wishes You'd sent somebody else to my rescue. I loved him so much when I was younger. He was my whole world, even though he never thought of me that way. Right now, I need to be focused and wise if I'm going to get through this. And I can't let any part of my mind, let alone my heart, be distracted by feelings for Lucas right now.

Darcy rolled over, wrapped a blanket around her and stared through the darkness in the direction of Lucas's family home. As country neighbors, their houses were so far apart that during the day, she couldn't see it through the trees. But at night, she'd always been able to see the distant light from Lucas's bedroom window from hers, and had often fallen asleep staring at its gentle glow, knowing he was there. She still slept in her large childhood bedroom, so that her parents could stay in their old familiar room when they visited But tonight the light in Lucas's childhood room was dark. Guess he'd stopped sleeping with a night-light on.

She'd been so upset with him for cutting her out of his life when she was sixteen and not reaching out to her. But could she have done more to repair the rift?

She'd been so incredibly angry...

She caught ahold of the thought as it flew across her mind.

No, that wasn't entirely honest. She hadn't been angry so much as she'd felt embarrassed, hurt, shocked, humiliated and rejected. And lashing out at him had somehow made her feel better.

Lord, do I owe Lucas an apology?

But Lucas had been the one who'd kissed her and then broken her heart. She couldn't remember a time before knowing Lucas and thinking that he was the most important friend in her life. At first he'd been that bigger and stronger older brother type, who'd let her sit next to him on the school bus and lent her all the best adventure books. The one day, when she'd been thirteen, she'd suddenly glanced at him sideways when they'd been sitting on the couch watching television, and felt something unexpected flutter in her chest.

She'd been fourteen when she'd first admitted to her diary that she had a crush on him. Sixteen when she'd gotten up the courage to admit her feelings to him.

She'd never expected that the moment she did he'd dash across the country and vanish from her life.

And now, the last thing she wanted to do was be vulnerable and open any part of her heart up to him again, even if it was just admitting how hurt she'd felt when he'd left and that she'd been wrong to blow up at him the way she did.

Sleep came slowly and fitfully. Darcy tossed and turned as she chased her fears and worries down with prayers to God for help.

Red alarm clock numbers told her it was shortly after two in the morning, when suddenly a dim light flicked on from somewhere inside her room. Darcy blinked, slowly at first, only to be jolted awake when she saw the large figure standing at the end of her bed. His face was shrouded by a hoodie. The flame of a cigarette lighter flickered in his hand, illuminating his form in the darkness. Panic poured like cold water over Darcy's limbs. Her heart beat painfully in her chest. But when she opened her mouth to scream, she was too terrified to make a sound.

"Hellllo, hoooney," Blaze said. "Ready to play another game?"

FOUR

She sat up in bed, petrified, as her eyes adjusted to the dim light and her mind battled what she was seeing. It couldn't be real. This hooded man now standing at the end of her bed had to be a dream, a nightmare from the most terrifying recesses of her mind.

Help. Me. Lord.

He was taller and broader than she remembered her attacker being. His form seemed to loom over the end of her bed, with his face hidden in the large hood of his sweatshirt. For a moment, he just stood there, menacing, still and shrouded in darkness, as if wanting to see her shake and force her to guess what was going to happen next. And even though her mind knew that it had to be a copycat, because the original Blaze—Robby Lamb—was dead and gone.

"Hello again, Darcy." Blaze's voice seemed to echo around her, taunting her. "Did you miss me?"

Instinctively, she curled her arms and legs into her chest, pulling the blankets up around her. But not like she was cowering. No. More like a cornered animal who was tensing up and getting ready to strike.

"You do like solving riddles, don't you, Darcy?" Blaze asked. It was unsettling how he kept saying her name. Again, he was still standing there. Not moving, just taunting. "You think you're smart, with your little mind whirring away, figuring things out?"

Darcy's fingers brushed against her phone, hidden somewhere in the folds of her bedding. It slipped from her fingers and fell to the floor. Her eyes darted to the side. The lamp was too far away to reach, but there was a mug of water on the nightstand.

The hooded figure didn't seem to notice.

"What happens next is all your fault, Darcy," Blaze said. "It was your riddle to solve. Tick tock, tick tock."

"Who are you?" Darcy shouted. Her voice sounded more like a panicked lamb's bleat than a lion's roar. But it was hers, and she was thankful she'd found it.

No answer from him.

"What do you want?" Her voice rose.

"Are you scared?" Blaze asked, ignoring her questions. "You should be."

Yes. She was terrified.

And she wasn't going to let the fear win. All she needed to do was keep Blaze talking until she was able to reach her phone and call for help. She'd fought with all her might against the chair she'd been tied to in the basement. And she'd fight again now.

Lord, what do I do? Do I stall him? Do I fight? Please, give me the strength I need to make it out of here alive.

Blaze began to laugh. A flame in his hand seemed to grow larger and brighter.

Something inside Darcy told her that it was now or never. She lunged for the bedside table, snatched the mug off it and threw it at Blaze as a distraction. Then she practically hurled herself off the bed and onto the floor. She hit the hardwood and scrambled for her cell phone, barely managing to snatch it before rolling under the bed. The screen of icons filled her eyes. She hit the red square that Gemma had installed, praying it would work and that help would come. Crackling laughter grew louder until it seemed to be coming from all around her. She couldn't see Blaze's feet anywhere. Had he climbed onto the bed? Was he blocking the door or hiding somewhere, waiting to strike? She crawled deeper under the bed—before he could dive beneath it, grab her ankles and try to pull her out.

Then a loud and deafening bang shook the room. A light flashed before her eyes that was so bright it temporarily blinded her. Then she smelled smoke.

He'd detonated some kind of explosive device. Her home was going to go up in flames. The only thing that mattered now was making it out alive.

God, please save me!

She crawled out from under the bed, sprinted across the floor and dove for the window that she'd left open a crack, without even letting herself look back. Darcy yanked the window up so hard she felt her fingernails break. Her phone was still clutched in her other hand, and she expected at any moment to feel a bullet or knife in her back or a ligature around her throat.

Instead, Blaze just laughed. The thick smell of smoke suddenly filled her lungs. Darcy pushed the window open and tumbled out headfirst, landing in the dirt on her hands and knees. Only then did she realize she was still in her socks. She scrambled up and ran through the dark woods toward Lucas's home, barely even feeling the rocks and rough ground beneath her feet or the branches smacking against her body.

Her family house had been invaded. Her home had been set on fire.

Yet she couldn't hear Blaze chasing her.

Why? Had he let her go?

Was he just biding his time before he grabbed her again?

Everything inside her wanted to turn and look back at the fire now consuming her home. But instead, she pushed herself forward, running as fast as her aching legs and lungs would allow. For a long, agonizing moment, the forest seemed to spread out dark, empty and silent ahead of her. She was alone, with no one to help her, no home to return to, and a ruthless criminal set on terrorizing her and taking her life.

She heard a dog barking and someone crashing through the trees toward her.

"Darcy!" Lucas shouted.

"I'm here!" she called back.

A moment later, she felt the soft and comforting bulk of Michigan brush against her legs. Then Lucas reached Darcy. His strong arms wrapped around her, and he pulled her into his chest. She shook against him.

"Are you okay?" he asked. His voice was husky, and she could feel his cheek resting on the top of her head as he held her close.

"Yeah, I'm okay." She leaned into him, allowing him to comfort her for just a moment.

"What happened?" Lucas asked. "I heard the alarm sound, and I came as fast as I could."

"It was Blaze." The name slipped from her lips as a whimper. "He set my house on fire. There was some kind of detonation and I smelled smoke…"

Her voice trailed off as she felt Lucas loosen his hold.

"What?" he asked. He sounded confused.

"Didn't you hear the explosion?" She pulled out of his arms. Only then did she finally let herself look back through the trees at her house, expecting to see a tower of orange flames and billowing smoke reaching up into the sky. Instead, all she saw were the dark silhouettes of trees. The smoke had faded from her lungs, and all she could smell was the cool night air and the comforting scent of Lucas beside her.

"I didn't hear any explosion," Lucas admitted, "and I don't see a fire."

His fingers brushed the sides of her face. "Are you sure that's what happened? Finnick said to doubt everything we think we know."

His touch was tender, but she pulled away from it.

Was she sure that the Blaze copycat had set her house on fire? Or that he'd broken into her home?

"Of course I'm sure," she said. "I heard the bang and I smelled the smoke."

What's happening?

A deep growl came from the darkness beneath her feet. Then Michigan barked sharply.

"Well, there's our answer," Lucas said. "Michigan agrees with you. My K-9 partner is telling me she detects a fire."

"You've got to believe me," Darcy said. Her voice sounded urgent, bordering on anxious. "I woke up to find Blaze standing at the end of my bed—"

"What?" Lucas's voice rose. He'd been in her bedroom watching her sleep? Lucas's heart was pounding so hard that for a moment, he could barely breathe. "How? What happened? Are you okay?"

"I'm fine," she said. She took a deep breath and then looked down at Michigan. His K-9 partner was still alerting toward her house. "He just taunted me, and then there was the detonation and smoke."

And yet they couldn't see any flames, and Michigan seemed to be the only one who detected fire. Then again, his K-9 was also trained to detect accelerants like gasoline, diesel fuel and even lighter fluid. It could be any one of those that Michi was reacting to.

"He was laughing at me," Darcy went on, "and talking. It was so creepy. It was like he wanted to scare me."

An involuntary shiver ran down Lucas's spine at the thought. He swallowed hard.

"I'm glad you're okay. Let's get back to my house and re-group," he said. In a moment he'd call his team, and they'd alert the authorities—right now he just wanted Darcy as far away from here as possible. "You can fill me in there. I'm going to contact the team and let them know I've got you and you're okay."

I've got you.

He hadn't really thought the words through when they'd come out of his mouth. But now, as he heard himself speak them, they hit him deeply, in a way he didn't quite understand and couldn't afford to think about at the moment. He signaled Michigan to his side.

"Good job," he told his partner. "Drop it."

"Drop it?" Darcy asked.

"It means to ignore the scent she's detected and move on," he explained. The K-9 pawed the ground in frustration, making it clear that she didn't want to drop the scent but would follow orders. She repositioned herself close by his right side. Then Lucas quickly dialed Finnick's cell phone number as they turned back toward his house and started walking.

Gemma answered.

"Hey," she said. The sound of a moving vehicle rumbled in the background. "We got Darcy's alarm notification, and I'm with Finnick in his truck. You're on speaker. We're heading your way now."

"Hello," Finnick's voice sounded in the background, along with Nippy woofing in greeting.

"We've got law enforcement and first responders en route to Darcy's now," Gemma said. "Tell me you've got good news."

"I do," Lucas said. "I've got Darcy with me now. She's safe."

He heard Finnick exhale and Gemma whisper a prayer of thanksgiving.

"The Blaze copycat broke into her house and set off some kind of explosive device," Lucas went on.

"Did she get a look at his face?" Finnick cut in.

"No."

"What kind of explosive device?" Gemma asked.

"We don't know," Lucas said. "There are a lot of unknowns."

He could hear the faint sound of sirens approaching, and he quickened his footsteps.

"Tell law enforcement that the intruder might still be on-site," Lucas said. "There also might be a fire—not that we can see flames from here. Again, information is limited. We're on foot."

He realized that Darcy wasn't keeping pace with him and looked back. She was gingerly making her way across the rough ground a few feet behind him, with Michigan lagging slightly behind him, too, as if checking in on her. Darcy was also limping. He stopped and waited for her to catch up.

Lucas covered the phone's mouthpiece. "Darce, are you okay?"

She nodded. "Yeah, I'm fine."

He wasn't sure that was true.

"I've got to wrap this up," he said, returning to the call, "and get out of the woods."

"Got it," Gemma said. "Caleb's about five minutes out from Darcy's. We're about twenty. We've been coordinating information with the local cops on the case."

Something in her tone hinted at the fact that local law enforcement might not be all that thrilled to be coordinating with the Cold Case Task Force, and he remembered what Finnick had said about being prepared to battle for jurisdiction.

"Anything I need to worry about there?" Lucas asked.

"The only thing you need to worry about right now is taking care of Darcy," Finnick said. "Sit tight until one of us can check in."

"Will do," Lucas said. "Thanks."

"No problem," Finnick said.

Lucas ended the call and then shone the dim light of the cell phone toward Darcy, and realized for the first time that she was in her socks.

"Where are your shoes?"

It was an instinctive question. But he could tell by the way her chin lifted that something about it rubbed her the wrong way.

"At my house." Defiance shone in her huge, dark eyes. "Obviously, I didn't go looking for them when a killer broke in and set my place on fire."

He winced slightly. Yeah, it might've been a dumb question, but she didn't need to snap back at him.

"I'm sorry." His hands rose. "I was just asking, not attacking. I'll carry you the rest of the way."

He slid his phone into his jacket pocket and reached out his hands, planning to pick her up. But instead, she stepped back.

"I'm okay," she said. "I don't need you carrying me like some helpless damsel in distress."

He was about to argue when a slight hitch in her voice made him stop.

She was scared, she was hurt and she was putting on a

brave face. The least he could do was show her some compassion and not take it personally.

"Honestly, Darce—" his voice dropped "—I've never once thought you were helpless. You're probably the least helpless person I've ever met. Truth is, sometimes you intimidated me by how strong you are."

He heard her gasp in the darkness.

"Really?" she asked.

"Yeah," he admitted. "Also, I'm pretty definitely distressed right now. I mean, who wouldn't be in distress about everything that's going on?"

To his surprise, she actually laughed. The sound warmed something deep inside his heart. He'd always loved making her laugh.

"Well, I've always thought you were incredibly strong too," she said. "But it's not like a brute-strength thing. You have this way of being strong that's also gentle and kind."

Gentle and kind strength, huh?

He swallowed hard. "Thank you." He'd never been described that way—certainly not by his dad. He realized how much he'd missed her friendship over the years. She'd been such a big part of his childhood. And yet...he couldn't let her make him feel this way. He was here in Sunset to help his dad and excel at his job. He could protect her, but he couldn't fall for her.

"You're welcome," Darcy said. "And yeah, I keep stubbing my toe, so if you don't mind, I'd love a piggyback ride."

Not quite the same as sweeping her up in his arms like he'd offered. But, then again, it was probably a safer option, considering his determination to keep his feelings for her at bay.

"Sure thing," he said. "Hop on."

He turned his back to her and crouched. He felt her hands

brush his shoulders, and then her weight fell against him as she settled onto his back. He scooped her up and began to jog toward his house. Immediately, he realized his mistake. Darcy's arms were wrapped around his neck, her cheek brushed against his face and the smell of her filled his senses—then the butterflies that had begun to flutter in his chest told him that he was nowhere near as over his youthful attraction to her as he liked to think he was.

The sound of his own heartbeat filled his ears, mingling with the sound of his feet pounding across the ground as he ran home with Michigan by his side. Minutes later, the trees parted and he could see the warm light of his front porch. He jogged toward his SUV, popped the trunk and stood back while it rose slowly. Then he turned around and set Darcy down on the edge with her legs dangling over the side. The yellow light of the vehicle shone down over her, enveloping her in its glow.

"Hang on," he said.

He reached past her into the back of his SUV, pulled out his gym bag, and then grabbed a pair of white gym socks, his extra sneakers, a soft hand towel and a water bottle.

"Here," he said. "These'll help you get turned around. I've got a sweatshirt, too, if you're chilly. It'll all be too big for you, but I figure it's better than nothing. Now, catch your breath, take a moment and then you can fill me in on everything that happened with Blaze. We're safe at my house, and law enforcement will be all over the crime scene. We have nowhere to rush off to, and they've got it covered. When you're ready, I'll record your statement so we can play it back for the team."

"Sounds good, thanks. Is your dad back here yet? Or is he still in hospital?"

"Hospital," Lucas said. "But he should be discharged first thing tomorrow."

"Have you talked to him yet?"

Darcy took a swig from the water bottle. Then she poured some water over the towel.

"Not yet," Lucas said.

It was a conversation he was both looking forward to and dreading.

"Thanks for letting me clean up before I see the others," she said. "I feel like I'm covered in dirt from running through the woods."

"Well, you don't look it," he said. He hesitated, standing in front of her for a moment. Then he sat on the far side of the trunk. It shifted under his weight. "I mean, I've seen you far worse. Remember that time we were climbing around the shore by the lookout point and you fell off a rock right into the water? You were so covered in mud I could barely figure out where your eyes were."

She laughed and whipped the end of the towel at him. "It was slippery," she said. "And you fell in too."

"You pulled me in!" he countered, his voice rising with a laugh. "When I was trying to pull you out!"

"Are you saying you let a little girl like me overpower you?" She batted her eyelashes at him. His breath caught for a moment—she was so beautiful and talking to her had always been so easy.

He smiled, then protested, "Only because you tricked me by acting helpless."

Darcy laughed even louder. She had no idea how much he'd missed that sound. *Stop that.* She pulled off her wet, dirty socks and slid on his fresh pair. They were so big on her they practically swallowed her feet and came halfway up to her knees.

"I'll take the sweatshirt too," she said. "I'm sorry. I should've thought ahead and had shoes and jacket ready in case I needed it."

"You had no reason to expect someone would break into your house," Lucas said, firmly. "You could just as easily blame me for not insisting you come stay with Michigan and me until all this settles over."

At least he knew his dad was still safe in the hospital.

He reached for the gray sweatshirt in his gym bag and wrapped it around her shoulders. Red and blue emergency lights flickered in the darkness now, above the tree line, as first responders surrounded Darcy's home.

Lord, please help law enforcement catch Blaze and end this nightmare.

He set his phone up to record a voice memo and then held it between them while Darcy told the story of how she'd woken up to see Blaze standing at the end of her bed.

"Logically, I know it has to be a copycat," Darcy said after describing what he'd looked like to the best of her memory. "But it looked just like him. His stance was identical, down to the slope of his shoulders. Only he seemed larger maybe? I'm not sure. I was in the bed and he was standing over me. And Robby was always a big guy."

"Well, you'd woken up," Lucas said. "You were terrified—also, the light was pretty low."

"Yeah." She nodded, but she didn't seem convinced. "Something just feels off about the whole thing, as if I'm not remembering it right."

Darcy slid the sweatshirt on. The soft fabric swamped her form.

"The whole time he had this lighter in his hand. I didn't have a weapon handy or any way to fight back. I wish I'd thought of that in advance too. So I just threw a mug at him to cause a distraction. Then I dove onto the floor and rolled under the bed."

"And then?" Lucas asked.

"Then there was an explosion."

"And you didn't see an explosive device?"

"No," she said. "All I saw was a bright light, heard a loud bang and smelled smoke. Then I sprinted for the window, climbed out and ran for my life. I didn't stop and look back."

Darcy pulled her legs up into her chest, until her heels were resting on the back of the truck. She wrapped her arms around herself.

"I'm so sorry," he said.

Instinctively, Lucas reached out toward her. For a moment he hesitated, with his hand hovering just inches away; then he let it drop onto her shoulder. Gently, he patted the back of her shoulder, silently letting her know that he was there for her and that she wasn't alone. She leaned into his touch for a long moment.

Then she pulled away and opened her eyes.

"This whole thing is so humbling," Darcy said. "If I was at work and somebody called in with this story, part of me would probably be secretly frustrated at how little they could tell me. Maybe I'd even judge them for it. You're being incredibly understanding about this."

She ran both hands through her short blond hair and let the wisps fall through her fingers. Then she reached over and paused the recorder.

"When I was first convinced that Robby Lamb was Blaze," she went on, "I ran to you and babbled out this long stream of consciousness. You listened. You took it seriously and went to your dad. Then today, when I felt like nobody was taking the threat of this new Blaze seriously, somehow I knew you'd listen, even though we hadn't spoken in years."

She looked down at her feet, still dangling several inches off the ground.

"To be honest," she continued, "I don't really remember our last conversation that well. I know I was upset and probably said some pretty harsh things. And I wish—"

Suddenly her words were swallowed up by the sound of a truck pealing down his gravel driveway as if its back tires were on fire. Lucas braced his hand to block the glare of the headlights.

He heard an engine cut, a door open and slam closed, and then footsteps running toward them. Then the headlights switched off and he saw Caleb.

"Lucas! Darcy!" Caleb called. His voice was cheerful, despite the undeniable hint of urgency. "Can we head inside and have a quick chat?"

"What's going on?" Lucas stood. Darcy shoved her feet into his spare pair of sneakers and hopped off the SUV after him. Michigan wagged her tail at Caleb in greeting.

"Corporal Austin Dillon is on his way over here to take Darcy's statement," the blond officer said. "I think he's planning on springing it on you, Darcy. Catch you off guard to see if he can trip you up. I just wanted to give you a heads-up, in case we all wanted to pop inside the house and figure out who should handle this."

There was a frankness to his voice that Lucas appreciated. Like a fellow boater flagging them down to warn them of a storm up ahead before it was too late to turn back.

"Catch me off guard about what?" Darcy demanded.

"They didn't find any sign of a break-in," Caleb said, "or of a fire or explosive device. I think he suspects that you made it up."

FIVE

That just wasn't true, Lucas thought. It couldn't be. Darcy might be an emotional person, but she wasn't foolish, a liar or the kind of person who'd mistake a nightmare for reality.

Before he could jump to her defense, Darcy was already stepping forward.

"Well, that's ridiculous," she said. "Obviously there was a break-in, and I'm not going to go hide in Lucas's house while people accuse me of things I didn't do."

"Okay," Caleb said and stepped back. His hands rose. "I'm not advising you to contact your lawyer or anything. I'm just saying that you have the right to make him wait until tomorrow if you want to talk to the task force first. After all, Finnick's willing to battle for jurisdiction on this one."

"Darcy has already given me her statement," Lucas said, "and Michigan detected a fire in the direction of Darcy's home."

But a second pair of headlights was coming down the gravel driveway now, which Lucas presumed had to be Austin's. The local cop was arriving so soon after Caleb had that Lucas realized Caleb must've booked it at full speed out of the scene to beat him here. But whatever Caleb's motivation had been, it was all for nothing, since Darcy strode across the driveway to meet Austin's squad car even as the officer was cutting the brakes.

His first impulse was to follow her, but when Caleb gestured subtly toward the house, Lucas followed the other officer's lead, signaled Michigan to his side and strode over to the porch.

"So, are you here to take my statement?" Darcy asked Austin. Her voice was loud and her tone was defiant. "Because this new Blaze copycat just broke into my home, threatened my life and needs to be caught?"

Lucas couldn't catch what Austin said in response. But there was no missing the arrogant smirk on his square face as Darcy launched into an impassioned breakdown of everything that had happened tonight.

"She doesn't intimidate easily, does she?" Caleb said, quietly.

"No, she doesn't." Lucas chuckled. Then he sighed and leaned back against the porch railing. Caleb stood to his left, Michigan sat down beside Lucas, and all three of them watched as Darcy gave her statement. "It was kind of you to have her back."

And more than a bit surprising. In the past few weeks since Lucas and Caleb had been working together, the slightly older officer had always come across as incredibly professional and competent, but also pretty cynical.

"I'm here to have *your* back," Caleb admitted, wryly. "Not hers. I know we haven't worked together that long, but you're a member of my team, and I'm always going to do my best to support you. I'm sure the others would say the same."

"Thank you," Lucas said, feeling a little overwhelmed by the unexpected vote of confidence. But very thankful, too, and maybe even slightly relieved.

"No problem," Caleb said. "Although, I'll admit I wish I

could've better observed Darcy's reaction to learning there's no evidence of a break-in. I'm not sure I fully trust her, and something tells me Finnick is more skeptical of her story than he lets on."

Lucas wasn't sure what to make of that. They continued to watch as Darcy gave her statement to the smirking cop.

"Is she always this fiery?" Caleb asked.

"Always," Lucas admitted, "especially when she thinks she's not being taken seriously. It's like she was so used to being one of the shortest kids in her class that she never had any clue just how ferocious and intimidating she can be when she wants to."

Caleb nodded thoughtfully, and Lucas had the suspicion that the other officer was thinking through things that he wasn't saying. They watched Austin shake his head at Darcy as if she was a confused little child. Darcy's arm-waving became more animated in response. Then Caleb turned away from them and lowered his voice further.

"The nerve of that guy," Caleb said, "Really. I mean, you're here interviewing a distraught witness, and Officer Smug decides he's going to swoop in for some surprise questioning to try to catch your witness out on a crime that you haven't been briefed on? Like I'm going to let that happen. What's Corporal Austin Dillon's story?"

"He's always been a jerk and a bully," Lucas said. "But the kind that's smart and doesn't get caught. We went to different high schools, and he had a reputation for knowing how to hit an opposing player without causing bruises."

"And now he's a cop," Caleb said with disgust. "Do you think we should look into him for the Blaze thing?"

Lucas blinked.

"For the crime eight years ago or the copycat now?" Lucas asked.

"Either or both," Caleb said. "I mean, he seems really determined to ignore the task force's jurisdiction."

"That could just be ego," Lucas said.

"Is it possible that he set the original fires, framed Robby Lamb and then killed him?" Caleb pressed.

"Not impossible," Lucas admitted, "but honestly the thought has never crossed my mind. Darcy made a pretty compelling case for Blaze being Robby, and my dad definitely seemed confident in Robby's confession."

"Could Austin be the copycat Blaze now?" Caleb asked.

"Possible," Lucas said. "After all, Austin would have connections and resources as a cop that the average person wouldn't. But what we're missing is motive. I mean, somebody has gone to a lot of trouble to mess with Darcy, not to mention also threatening my dad's life and burning down his house."

"And wasted a lot of law enforcement resources," Caleb added.

"That too," Lucas agreed. "And why would he do that?" Why would anybody do that?

"You're not listening—" Darcy's voice rose suddenly "—and I'm done trying to explain things to you."

She turned and started back down the driveway toward the house, where Lucas and Caleb were standing.

"Lying to police and abusing law enforcement services are a crime," Austin called after her. "There's no shame in admitting you had a nightmare or got scared of a shadow and overreacted."

"I know!" Darcy snapped back. "But lying to a victim to get them to falsely confess is a crime too!"

She stormed over to Lucas and Caleb, the oversize shoes kicking up dirt as she went.

"Actually," Caleb said, softly, "cops are allowed to lie to

witnesses." There was a slight warning edge to his voice. "So keep that in mind in case someone is trying to frame you for something."

Immediately, Darcy's eyes fixed on Lucas's face. "Is that true?"

"Unfortunately," Lucas said.

"Huh." Darcy blinked. "Well, that sucks."

He glanced past her to where Austin was now climbing into his cop car and pulling out. The officer was scowling.

"Have you ever lied to a witness or suspect to solve a crime?" Darcy asked Caleb.

The blond officer shook his head.

"Never," Caleb said, simply.

"Good," Darcy said. "Because I wouldn't be able to trust you if I knew you had."

Before anyone could say anything further, Lucas's and Caleb's phones pinged simultaneously. Lucas glanced at the screen. It was Gemma, letting them know that she and Finnick were at Darcy's house and that law enforcement were beginning to pack up and head out.

Lucas breathed a silent sigh of relief.

It was time to get the investigation back on track.

Caleb suggested they drive back to Darcy's house together, due to just how many law enforcement vehicles he said were around Darcy's house and how tricky it would be for the larger ones to get in and out. Lucas agreed immediately, mostly because he wasn't quite sure he wanted to be alone with Darcy right now. Sitting alone with her on the back of the SUV had felt too much like old times. Back when they'd been best friends and he'd been trying very hard to fight the fact that his heart wanted something more.

And the last thing he, Darcy or this case needed right now

was for him to spend one moment longer thinking about those days.

They drove over together, with Darcy in the front seat beside Caleb and Lucas in the back beside Michigan. Caleb's back window was open a crack, and Lucas watched his partner carefully as Michigan sniffed the night air. The dog no longer seemed to be detecting anything, which was odd, as the scent of fire and accelerants could linger in the air for a long while.

When the turnoff for Darcy's house came into view, Caleb stopped the car, and they watched as a slow parade of emergency vehicles left her driveway and disappeared into the night, including two fire trucks, two cop cars and an unmarked police car. As Caleb turned into Darcy's lane, he saw a single ambulance waiting by the side of the driveway, in front of her car and Finnick's truck. Caleb flashed his headlights at it in greeting and waved out the window, as if to tell the ambulance that all was good and they were free to leave. The ambulance flashed its lights in return and then drove past them into the night.

Finnick, Nippy and Gemma met them on the front porch. Then, after a quick briefing from Finnick, the Cold Case Task Force split up and began to search Darcy's property. Gemma walked Darcy through the home, looking for anything that had been moved or was amiss. Finnick searched all the entrances and exits while Caleb covered the outside perimeter and Lucas instructed Michigan to search for any sign of fire.

The search was thorough, slow and meticulous—and it came up frustratingly empty. With the exception of a few trampled branches outside the bedroom window where Darcy had leaped out, the mass of footprints and tire tracks from emergency responders, and the mug that Darcy had hurled across her bedroom, there was no clear sign that anything had happened there that night.

The only thing that anyone had been able to find that was even a little out of the ordinary were three small round indentations that Caleb had found in the soft earth near the side of the house.

"Unless Blaze also happens to be a peg-legged pirate, that doesn't tell us much," Caleb told Finnick and Lucas dryly as they reconvened on the porch and compared notes. "But I photographed them and I'm sure if they mean anything, Gemma will find them."

"If there's something to find, she'll find it," Finnick agreed.

His boss sent Caleb inside to join Gemma and brief her and Darcy. Lucas couldn't hear any of their words but could catch enough of Darcy's tone to know she wasn't happy with the fact the team hadn't found anything.

"I want you and Caleb to take shifts watching Darcy for the rest of the night," Finnick told Lucas. The two of them stood side by side on Darcy's front porch with Michigan and Nippy. Lucas wondered why Finnick had asked to speak to him alone outside. "It seems there's been two attempts on Darcy's life so far today and I don't want to risk her being alone for a third. Tomorrow, after we've all gotten some sleep, we'll regroup and figure out how to keep her and your father safe."

"She and Caleb can stay at my place," Lucas said. "It's a huge farmhouse, and I've got plenty of rooms, even after Dad gets home tomorrow... You still believe her, right?"

Finnick sighed and ran his hand over his gray hair.

"Honestly?" Finnick asked. "My mind doesn't know what to believe. My brain thinks she still isn't telling the whole truth. Which is not the same as thinking she's lying. Yet my gut tells me there's somebody after her, who's either trying to drive her insane or make people seriously doubt her sanity."

Darcy was having a nightmare. She was standing backstage at her old high school. Somehow she was sixteen years old again and listening to Robby Lamb do magic tricks in the spotlight in front of a packed crowd. Lucas was standing behind her. His hand was on her shoulder, like it had been when they were sitting on the back of the SUV. Lucas's fingers brushed along the side of her jaw and tangled in her hair.

She reached for him, but instead her right hand was gripped around the rough wooden frame of a prop door she'd built when she was eighteen. Which didn't make sense, because Robby had been dead by then and Lucas had been gone. But then why was she sixteen again?

Something was wrong. Everything was wrong.

"It's a trick doorframe," she started telling Lucas. "It uses hidden mirrors, and there's a trapdoor beneath the stage to make it look like an actor vanishes the moment they step through."

But then his fingers grabbed ahold of her shoulder so tightly she cried out in pain. She tried to wriggle out of his grasp, but then suddenly, he was gripping her neck and squeezing the air from her body.

She screamed again, and then somehow she was facing him.

And it wasn't Lucas—it was Blaze.

The hood of his disguise loomed over her like a mouth ready to swallow her whole.

She grabbed the hood and yanked it back off his face.

And awoke from the dream to find herself sitting upright in an unfamiliar bed with bright morning sunshine streaming through the window. Her eyes darted around the room, from the plaid shirts hanging on the back of the door and the shelves of adventure novels and police procedural books to the rows of small sports trophies and medals that hung neatly in the trophy cabinet across from the window.

Her hand rose to her chest, and she pressed her palm against her racing heart as the memories of the day and night before began to filter back into her mind. She was safe in Lucas's childhood bedroom, with Lucas and his colleague Caleb sleeping in shifts downstairs.

Thank You, Lord, that Lucas was there for me when I needed him and that he took me seriously. Thank You that, despite how scared and unsettled I feel, I'm not alone.

At least, she was as long as she kept the past at bay and didn't let it interfere with this case and what was going on now. There'd been something so comforting and familiar about sitting with Lucas on the back of the SUV.

But then, once the team had shown up, Finnick has assigned Gemma and Caleb to brief her while he talked with Lucas alone. She had no doubt that Lucas would continue to do his job as a cop. But would he be there for her as a friend?

More importantly, would he continue to stand up for her against his team when they disagreed with her?

If she leaned on him and counted on him to be there for her, to be in her corner, would he let her down again?

She couldn't afford to let her emotional guard down with Lucas. Not now. Not with her life on the line and this new Blaze copycat on the loose.

As much as she might've liked feeling his hand on her shoulder and the warmth of his sweatshirt wrapped around her.

She heard a gentle whimper and felt something soft nudge her side. She looked down to see Michigan sitting on the floor beside her. The dog rested her large golden head on the bed beside Darcy.

"Good morning, Michigan," she said, softly feeling an unexpected lump form in her throat. "How did you get in here?"

The bedroom door was barely open a sliver. Darcy ran her hand over Michigan's soft head, feeling the dog's silky ears fall between her fingers.

The animal nuzzled her snout deeper into Darcy's hand and licked her fingers gently. Then Michigan trotted over to the bedroom door and worked it open with a combination of her snout and paws. Michigan slipped out into the hallway, then pushed the door shut behind her.

Darcy laughed. It was only then, as she reached for her phone on the bedside table, that she realized it was just after nine thirty. She checked her email and discovered that Simon, her supervisor, had sent her a message saying that he was sorry to hear about the "unfortunate incident" from the night before and that she could take the afternoon off work if she needed to take a personal day to recover. Darcy fired back a quick message telling him that she was fine and she'd see him that afternoon for her shift as usual. Then she took a deep breath, said a prayer and prepared herself to face the day.

The warm and inviting scent of coffee wafted up toward her as she made her way downstairs.

But any hope she might've had of starting the day with a casual meal over a soothing cup of coffee vanished when she found Lucas standing in the kitchen in his official K-9 uniform, with his dark hair slightly damp as if he'd rushed to get ready. He was pouring hot, steaming coffee into two mismatched travel mugs. Michigan was lying under the kitchen table, and she didn't see Caleb anywhere.

"Good morning," she said. "Did you know I woke up with Michigan beside my bed?"

Lucas chuckled lightly.

"Good morning," Lucas said. "Yeah, Michi is a pretty talented dog. As long as a door's not shut completely, she'll find a way to open it."

"I used to be into doing magic tricks," Darcy said, still feeling the nightmare she'd had lingering at the edges of her brain. "A bunch of the STAV kids were. I don't think Robby was, though." Despite how he'd appeared in her dream. "I still remember how to twist my hands to get out of handcuffs if they're not too tight. Maybe Michigan and I could do a double act."

Lucas laughed again. Then he looked back down at the coffees he'd just poured, and his smile disappeared.

"I'm sorry to rush you," he said, "but I just got a call from Gemma, tipping us off to the fact the high school is holding a special assembly this morning to address the Blaze 911 call that came in yesterday. Finnick thought it would be good to have a member of the task force present along with getting our perspective, as people who went to the high school when Robby Lamb was a student there."

He offered her one of the travel mugs. She took it so quickly she practically snatched it from his hand. It was as if she wanted to prevent herself from accidentally brushing her fingers against his and reigniting whatever weird spark in her brain had led to her dreaming about him the night before.

Last night's physical closeness had been both unexpected and familiar, but she wasn't about to let it happen again. Somehow, sitting beside Lucas on the back of the SUV...it was almost like their relationship had been reset back to that moment in the gazebo, overlooking the lake five years ago, just before she'd foolishly blurted out her feelings for him and he'd kissed her. The last thing she needed now was for either of them to start thinking about what had happened after that. Emotional closeness as old friends who trusted each other and were working together to stop a criminal was absolutely perfect. And this time she'd make sure they left it at that.

"Where's Caleb?" she asked.

Lucas broke away from her gaze. He added a dash of milk to his coffee and swished it around.

"He's off chasing some leads for Finnick," he said.

"What leads?"

"Don't worry about it," he said. "I'll make sure you're filled in on all the broad strokes of the investigation."

"Sure," she said, with a laugh that sounded a lot more forced than she'd intended it to. "But I like knowing all the nitty-gritty details."

"I know you do." Lucas was still looking at his coffee, like he was searching the beige and brown swirls for answers. "But it's pretty common not to brief witnesses on every lead that's being chased—only those that yield results. Rest assured the team is looking into a lot of different people's alibis."

Okay, she wasn't quite sure what to do with that.

"Did Gemma manage to track where Blaze texted me from, at least?" she asked.

"I don't have any details on that either," Lucas said. "Anyway, I'm sorry there's not much in the way of food. I did do a quick run to the corner store for some yogurt cups and prepackaged breakfast sandwiches. They're on the top shelf of the fridge."

He wasn't just avoiding her question—he was practically steamrolling over it.

"I'll brief you in the car as we go," he said. "Unless you'd rather take separate vehicles. But for now, I've got to get my head in the game, give Michigan a quick run and get her into her K-9 vest. Usually, the task force members are in plain clothes, but Finnick thought it might be good to show up in uniform. The school knows we're coming, but they're not exactly thrilled about it."

He shoved a lid down on the top of his mug, picked it up and headed for the kitchen door. Michigan stood and followed him. Then he hesitated with his hand on the door-frame.

"You going to be okay?" he asked.

"Oh, absolutely," she said. "I'm fine, and I'm good for us to travel together and talk then."

"Great." Lucas's smile in response was as unconvincing as hers felt. "I should be ready in ten."

"Awesome."

He disappeared through the door.

She opened the fridge, ignored the rubbery looking pre-made sandwiches and grabbed a strawberry yogurt. She found a spoon and stirred the thick mixture. Then she slumped into a chair, feeling strangely deflated but not quite sure why.

It wasn't like she'd had any reason to expect they'd start the day by sitting down together for a home-cooked meal of pancakes and bacon. But there'd been something so reassuring, comforting and almost empowering about the way that the Cold Case Task Force had taken her fears about the Blaze copycat seriously and seemed to rally around her the day before. And now, while Lucas wasn't sidelining her exactly, he definitely seemed far less chatty and open about the case than he had been.

Eight minutes and half a yogurt eaten later, Darcy and Lucas were back in his K-9 SUV, heading to the rural high school that lay on the opposite edge of Sunset. Despite his promise to loop her in when they were on their way, an uneasy silence filled the SUV between them. She glanced behind her to where Michigan sat proudly with her K-9 vest on. And Darcy couldn't help but notice that the golden Lab seemed to be the only one who was enthusiastic about the trip.

Lucas pulled to a stop at the town's only stoplight and waited for it to change. They'd been silent during the car ride, and she floundered for something to say.

"Did you hear from your dad today?" she asked.

"Not yet, but I expect to when they discharge him," Lucas said. After a moment, he added, "I'll settle him back into the farmhouse later." She nodded. "Why did you move into the bungalow with him instead of staying in the farmhouse?"

"My goal has always been to get him to move back with me," Lucas said. "But I didn't want to leave him there alone."

"So, if Ed moved out because of a falling-out with Marie, why didn't he move back into the farmhouse when Marie moved out?" Darcy asked. "Or am I missing something?"

"Whatever you're missing, I'm missing it too," Lucas said. "Maybe he didn't want to be surrounded by the memories of her. He now says he wants to get rid of all her stuff."

"Well, if it's any help, there's a great second-hand store in town called Shiny's that'll take everything, from furniture to clothes," she said. "I shop there a lot."

"Thanks." He shook his head. "The whole situation with him makes me feel so unbelievably helpless. Whatever's going on with him, he's completely shut me out. Every time I bring it up, he tells me that now's not the time and we'll discuss it later. But later never comes."

"I had no idea your relationship with your father was so

complicated," Darcy admitted. "I always found him intimidating, but he always seemed to like you."

"I did a pretty good job of staying on his good side." Lucas slowed as he eased the vehicle through the short blocks of stop signs on Sunset's old Main Street. "Dad was always charming. Big voice. Bigger personality. I can see why he was a good fire chief and people wanted him to run for mayor. And there definitely seemed to be a genuine tenderness between him and Marie. But he was never a warm and fuzzy kind of dad who talked about feelings. More like, he saw his role as setting high standards for me and pointing out when I failed to meet them."

She knew Ed expected a lot from him, but she'd never picked up on how intense that must've been for Lucas, and he likely wouldn't have talked about it had she asked. "I saw all the trophies and medals in your room," she said. "He must've been proud of those."

Lucas snorted. "I'm guessing you didn't read the small text on any of them," he said. "A lot of those are for personal achievements, second- and third-place finishes, completing major challenges or improvement and stuff like that. All the first-place wins are for team sports, and he didn't count team wins unless I was also MVP. Because team wins don't count, only individual victories."

He pulled the SUV out of the small town and onto a rural highway. Trees and farms streamed past the windows.

"Anyway, we should talk about the school thing," he went on. He was changing the subject, and despite how much her heart ached for him, she let him. They needed to focus on the case. "Honestly, we might be walking into a minefield of angry teachers and worked-up students. Students have been all over social media, spinning wild stories about Blaze being back. Gemma picked up online that the school has been dealing with a lot of drama so far this morning from parents, students and community members about the Blaze call yesterday. Not that they're going to know that you're the one who took that call—"

"Unless I tell them," Darcy interrupted.

Lucas clenched his jaw. "I don't suggest you do that," he said. "In fact, I'm bringing you as an observer, not to talk about the investigation. You're clearly being targeted by this guy, and the less attention you bring to yourself, the better. We don't want to paint an even bigger bull's-eye on your back."

She opened her mouth to interrupt.

"Apparently," he continued, "they're having an assembly to talk about civic responsibility and not misusing 911 or spreading rumors online. Finnick placed a call to the principal and told her that a member of the task force would be dropping by to talk about any concerns and be available if the staff or students have any questions. If this Blaze copycat's goal was to create drama, fear, misinformation and chaos, he's definitely winning that game."

"Well, except for the fact that whatever this attacker wants, his 'game' isn't about causing chaos or spreading rumors," Darcy jumped in. "It's much worse than that."

"We don't know that," Lucas said. "It might be about instilling fear in the town."

"Lucas, he broke into my house while I was sleeping and threatened me," Darcy said. "After taunting me, kidnapping me, drugging me, leaving me tied up in Ed's bungalow and setting the house on fire!"

She could hear a defensive edge in her voice, and she wasn't quite sure where it was coming from. After all, it wasn't as if any of this was news to Lucas.

"I get that," Lucas said, "but that doesn't mean that we

can guess what his ultimate goal is or what he's trying to accomplish."

"He threatened to burn down the school!" Darcy said. "The school shouldn't even be open!"

"According to *you*, he threatened to burn down the school," Lucas said. "Based on your ability to decipher his riddle. And as for all the other attacks, you're the only one who witnessed any of that."

She couldn't believe what she was hearing.

"You know that's what happened," Darcy said.

"I know that's what you *said* happened," Lucas said. His eyes were fixed on the road ahead. His hands gripped the steering wheel tightly. "And I believe you. But remember, my team didn't find any actual evidence that Blaze broke into your house last night. And we don't have any hard evidence that Blaze ever kidnapped you and tied you up in my dad's basement."

"You were there!"

"No, I wasn't," Lucas said. He stopped the SUV and she looked out the windshield to see they'd reached the high school parking lot. The plain redbrick walls of the long and sprawling two-story building where she'd spent hours of the longest years of her life filled her view. Then she turned back to Lucas. He was looking at her.

"I'm going to talk to you like a cop for a moment," Lucas said, "not as a friend. Because I know that as a 911 dispatcher, you've got to be pretty well acquainted with how law enforcement works, and I think you deserve to hear some blunt, hard truths. Okay?"

She took off her seat belt and turned toward him. "Fine." Bring it on.

"Nobody has seen this Blaze copycat but you," Lucas said. "Just you. I haven't even heard the 911 call yet, although I'm sure Gemma is working on getting a copy for our team to review. But even if we all agreed the voice was identical— which my father, the fire chief, disputes—you're still the one who figured out what his secret code meant—"

"But you saw me tied to that chair in the basement—" she cut in.

"No, I didn't," Lucas said, firmly. "I found you on the floor, tangled up in some rope and tied to the remains of a broken chair. I have absolutely no concrete proof that you didn't set the fire yourself and tie yourself to that chair. Do I?"

The words hit her like a punch in the gut. Yes, all right, all that was technically true. But how could he even say that? Instinctively, she reached toward him, not even pausing to think about what exactly she was reaching for or why. Her fingertips brushed the edge of his sleeve. His fingers caught ahold of hers, and for a long moment, he held her hand inside his. His green eyes locked on her face and something she couldn't decipher filled the depths of his eyes. Then, before she could even figure out what to say, he dropped her hand, cut the engine, turned around and signaled to Michigan.

"Come on, Michi!" he said. "Time to get to work!"

Lucas got out, opened the back door for his partner, waited for the K-9 to jump out and then clipped Michigan's leash onto her collar. While he lingered by the vehicle long enough to make sure that Darcy had gotten out all right and was joining them, once she slammed her door, he strode toward the school at a pace too quick to keep the conversation going.

She quickened her step to keep up. She'd never seen Lucas and Michigan in their official uniforms before. The duo made a handsome and impressive-looking pair.

She felt her hands clench into fists at her sides and forced herself to pray.

Help calm my heart, Lord. I don't like the questions Lucas was asking. I really want to argue with him right now, and I'm not even sure why. It's like I've got all this fight in me, and I don't know where to channel it.

Lucas paused at the front door of the school to hold it open for her, then continued purposefully toward the main office, holding on to Michigan's leash. Michigan trotted close to Lucas's side with her head high and nose sniffing the air intently. They stopped at the front office, where an elderly secretary, whom Darcy was pretty sure had been there back when they'd been students, told Lucas that the principal was currently in a meeting about finding the culprits behind a spate of false emergency calls that morning that had paramedics dashing up and down the halls, looking for a teenager who'd apparently collapsed. She added that an announcement would be made in a few minutes to send students to the auditorium for the assembly and that she'd get someone to escort them there.

Michigan's sniffing grew fiercer and more deliberate. Then the K-9 whined softly and pawed the floor. The office phone rang.

"We'll make our way there, thanks," Lucas said, quickly, as the secretary was reaching for the phone to answer it. Then he tugged Michigan's leash, turned and walked back out into the hallway before the secretary could respond, once again leaving Darcy to hurry to keep up.

Lucas paused just outside the office's front door and glanced from side to side. She followed his gaze. Long, empty high school hallways spread out in both directions, with a third one jutting away to their right.

Michigan whimpered again.

"Is everything okay?" Darcy asked.

"No." He leaned toward Darcy and his voice dropped. "Michigan detects arson."

SIX

Lucas bent down toward Michigan and said, "Show me."

Michigan woofed confidently and lifted her head to smell the air.

"There's a fire in the school?" Darcy asked, her voice rising. "We've got to sound the alarm and evacuate the place."

"Not yet," Lucas said, firmly. His hand rose toward her like a traffic cop, and there was an edge to his voice she'd never heard before. "Not until we actually know something and have any facts about what's going on."

Michigan barked again and tugged at the leash, leading them down the hallway to the right. Lucas walked beside his K-9 partner, with a tight hold on the leash and his eyes focused intently on every aspect of Michigan's body as the golden Lab searched the school.

"It's her job to detect and find things," Lucas went on. "It's mine to determine what they mean. For all we know, there's safe fire burning in a chemistry, woodshop or cooking class."

But the deep lines that furrowed his brow showed her that Lucas was worried that what Michigan was looking for could be something much worse. She followed their lead as Michigan guided them through the halls, deeper into the bowels of the school. Their footsteps echoed on the tile floors and seemed to bounce against the walls. Snippets of classes filtered in from the rooms on either side as they passed. Questions and concerns filled her mind. But both Lucas's and Michigan's full focus was intently locked on tracking something she could not see, taste or smell.

Lord, I have never been good at dragging my feet when people are in danger. Help them find whatever the potential risk is that Michigan is sniffing out. And help me to know what to do when they find it.

The dog's footsteps grew quicker, and Darcy felt her heart speed up inside her chest to keep pace. The faint smell of chlorine reached Darcy's senses now, no doubt from the school swimming pool. Then they reached the large double doors to the auditorium, where the student assembly would be held in a few minutes, and finally she could smell the faintest scent of gasoline fumes. Michigan pawed at the auditorium door and barked sharply.

The K-9's meaning was clear: *It's in here!*

"Stay behind me," Lucas told Darcy.

Lord, help us.

He pushed the door open and stepped inside, with Michigan at his heels. Darcy followed. The double doors swung shut and clicked behind them. A smattering of faces glanced in their direction. There were maybe two dozen high school students in the room. All older, she guessed, between the ages of seventeen and eighteen, and wearing black T-shirts with the same bright orange STAV logo, for the Stage, Tech and Audio Visual club that Darcy had belonged to when she was in high school. Most were setting up the chairs for the assembly. A few were on the stage, getting the sound system in place. A blonde girl who looked like she was in the graduating class was rehearsing a speech about how making fake 911 calls was a crime.

Most of the students glanced up at them. A few raised

their phones seemingly to take a picture of the adorable police dog who'd just walked into the room. But none of them looked particularly bothered or excited by the intruders. Lucas nodded in their direction, then he leaned toward Darcy.

"Michigan is pulling me toward the stage," he said. "Remind me, what's back there?"

"A very small backstage area," Darcy said. "Two dressing rooms and an exit door that leads to a hallway that's really only used by maintenance, not students."

"What's off the hallway?" he asked. "A supply closet or janitor's office with flammable liquids?"

"Yeah," she said, "all of the above, and also the garage for car maintenance class."

"Any of those could be it," Lucas said, softly.

A teenage girl sitting on the stage made a comment about the dog sniffing out another student's sandwich, and a couple of others laughed.

But as Darcy looked up at the familiar red velvet curtains, remnants of her nightmare began to flicker in the back of her mind, and all she felt was dread.

"Mr. Crockett just stepped out, if you're looking for him," a tall boy called from near the bleachers. Darcy paused and glanced back. The kid had floppy hair, that reminded Darcy of the 1960s, shoved under a baseball cap.

"Who's he?" she called.

"Teacher adviser for STAV Club," the kid replied. "STAV stands for Stage—"

"—Tech, Audio and Visual," Darcy cut him off. "Yeah, I know. I was club president in grade twelve."

"Cool." The kid nodded and turned to pull a stack of chairs out from under the bleachers. By the look of things, they were almost done setting up.

Suddenly, Michigan barked loudly and urgently. The

sound seemed to echo around the room, rebounding throughout the space. Darcy turned back and ran toward Lucas, who was standing at the stage steps. The dog was halfway up them, with her front paws braced on the stage and her nose pointed toward the catwalk directly above the students' heads. Darcy froze.

There, there, there! the dog's furious barks seemed to shout. *Urgent, urgent, urgent, urgent!*

"What's up there?" Lucas shouted.

"Nothing but the catwalk," she said. Definitely nothing the dog should be alerting to.

She looked up, her eyes peering into the gloom. A small rectangular box, roughly the size of a toolbox, sat on a metal beam high above their heads.

Was it an explosive device? If so, why hadn't it gone off yet?

In one quick move, Lucas reached for a fire alarm and yanked it hard. A loud, insistent ringing filled the air. He tucked Michigan's leash inside her K-9 harness so that the dog could move freely without dragging it behind her. Then he pulled his cell phone and held it to his ear.

"Dispatch! This is Officer Lucas Harper of the Ontario Cold Case Task Force," he yelled into the phone. "We have a 10-62 with a possible 400 at Meadowvale High School."

He started for the back of the room, with Michigan by his side and Darcy close behind. The dog had stopped barking, and Darcy realized he must have signaled to his K-9 partner to drop the scent at some point without her noticing.

"Again," he said, "this is Officer Harper, badge number 1-4-6-3-0-2-K-9-C. I've got a potential arson at Meadowvale High School with a possible explosive device. Dispatch a full emergency response—firefighters, paramedics and bomb squad. We need an evacuation."

He covered the phone with his hand and turned toward the auditorium. "Hey! This isn't a false alarm! Get out of here!"

Darcy looked back, expecting to see the students fleeing with the same urgency that she felt beating in her heart.

Instead, they were lingering, playing on their phones and stuffing things into their backpacks, as if this was no different than the dozens of other fire drills and false alarms they'd no doubt experienced in the past four years of high school, including yesterday. The trio of girls near the stage wasn't even moving, seeming more focused on filming what was going on around them.

Darcy leaped up on the stage and grabbed ahold of the microphone.

"This is real!" she shouted into the mic. Her amplified voice rose above the incessant ring of the wailing siren. "There's a fire! We need to get out of here."

The girls' faces paled.

"Is it Blaze?" one student called.

"The authorities will determine that. We need to evacuate—now!" Darcy shouted.

Voices rose in a cacophony of shouts and panicked conversation as students rushed for the door.

"Darcy, come on!" Lucas yelled. He'd stopped running and turned back to face her. "We've got to get everyone out of here!"

She leaped off the stage and ran toward him. But even as she did, she could see teenagers gathered around the closed auditorium exit. Students were shaking the push bars. Others were banging on the glass.

"Open the door!" Lucas yelled.

"It's locked!" one of the kids called. "We're locked in and can't get out!"

"There's another door behind the stage!" Darcy shouted.

Just then, a bang sounded behind them that seemed to shake the floor beneath their feet. Smoke and screams filled the air.

Darcy looked back to see fire raining down.

The catwalk had exploded. The back of the auditorium was in flames.

Lucas watched in horror as fire cascaded down from the ceiling above the stage, creating a curtain of flames blocking them off from the back exit. The main doors might be locked, but they were also the only way out. Sprinklers burst on above their heads, but he also knew from experience their role was to slow the fire down and buy the students enough time to escape. They wouldn't stop the building from burning down. Panicked voices rose around him as students banged on the locked doors, rattled the push bar and screamed for help.

"I'm locked in the auditorium with about a dozen students," Lucas shouted to dispatch. "The auditorium is on fire. I repeat, the auditorium is on fire and civilians are locked inside."

Then he ended the call, pocketed his phone and charged at the door.

"Out of the way!" he shouted, and the students parted in front of him as he ran toward the doors. He threw his full weight against it. The doors shuddered against his shoulder but didn't budge. He gasped a deep breath and tried again, only to feel searing pain fill his joints upon contact as the doors stubbornly refused to move. Now, through the tempered-glass window, he could see other students who'd noticed they were in trouble and were trying to yank the doors open from the outside.

He waved them away.

"Go!" Lucas shouted through the doors. "Get out of the building! Now!" He turned back to the students around him. "We're going to have to break the door down!"

He glanced around for anything they could use to bash their way out. A boy to his right raised a chair and tried to smash the window with one of the legs, barely managing to chip the reinforced glass. A girl to his left pulled what looked like a small but sharp defensive spike from her key chain.

With a start, Lucas realized that Darcy was no longer by his side.

"Darce?" he called. "Darcy?"

He searched the terrified and desperate students for her face. Finally, he saw her. Darcy was running away from him, toward, the fire-drenched stage.

What was she doing? Where was she going?

"Darcy!" he shouted. "Stop!"

She didn't even turn. Instead, she leaped back up onto the stage. For an agonizing moment, he saw her crouched there, silhouetted by the smoke that billowed around her and the bright orange flames now spreading down the curtains and across the ceiling above her.

Then she vanished.

His breath stopped. His sensible brain told him that his utmost responsibility was to get these teenagers out alive. But the heart beating hard in his chest made him want to practically hurl himself across the room to find and save her. Michigan whimpered. The dog's cry seemed to echo in Lucas's aching heart. The students had barely chipped the glass.

"Go for the hinges!" he yelled. "Don't stop, and don't look back! I'll be with you in a moment."

He signaled Michigan to his side and ran back toward the blinding wall of orange flames consuming the backstage. Smoke filled his eyes and seared his throat. He'd give himself a minute to look for her. No more. And if he couldn't find her, he'd have to let her go.

He'd barely run four steps when he saw her head and shoulders emerge from the stage. He blinked as his mind tried to process what he was seeing.

"Lucas!" Darcy shouted. "Send them this way! I've found a way out!"

"How?"

Two paces more and he could see she'd emerged from a trapdoor, hidden on the stage.

"We can go underneath the fire and come out the other side! I've tried it. The door's open!"

He didn't need to ask questions or know anything more. Darcy said there was a way out, and he believed her.

"This way!" he yelled at the students as he ran back toward the double doors. "There's a way out under the stage through the trapdoor!"

"I'm setting up a stepladder just underneath the hole!" Darcy's voice called from behind him. "It's a bit tricky to find a way out of here. I can't get the lights to work. But I can lead them out."

Michigan barked and ran around behind the students, helping Lucas as he herded them away from the locked doors and toward the stage. One by one, he watched as they disappeared through the trapdoor, trusting that Darcy was there and ushering them to safety on the other side. The fire spread above him, overwhelming the sprinklers and making its way down the walls. Flames and smoke filled the room until he could barely see the dark, square hole on the stage. He ran up the stage steps with Michigan by his side, as finally, the last student slipped into the dark space underneath the stage.

The trapdoor lay empty beneath him.

"Darcy!" he called down. "That's the last of them!"

Her face appeared below him, illuminated in the bright glow of her cell phone's flashlight.

Behind him, he could hear the wood at the side of the stage beginning to buckle and fall. "Are the students outside?"

"Mostly," she said. "I keep running back and forth from directing the front of the line to holding up the ladder."

"Go, get them out of here. Just move the ladder out of the way, I'll grab Michigan and be right behind you."

For a split second, her face lingered in the dark space. Her skin seemed to glow, and her hair was a golden frame around the beautiful lines of her face.

"Okay," she said, hesitating. "See you soon."

She disappeared, taking the light with her. Then all he saw was black. Fiberglass ceiling tiles bubbled and buckled as they crashed down onto the floor around him. He turned to his faithful K-9 partner. Michigan's trusting eyes were locked on his face.

Lucas patted his shoulders. "Michigan, jump!"

The dog leaped up on her hind legs and into Lucas's arms as he bent down to catch her. He scooped her up like an oversize toddler, with her front paws and head resting on his shoulder. Then he breathed a prayer and dropped straight down into the darkness. It was about a ten-foot drop. His feet landed safely on something soft, which he guessed was a thick foam crash mat. He set Michigan down on the ground and looked around, and for a moment, saw nothing but pitch black in all directions as his eyes struggled to adjust. The afterimage of the flames above still danced before his eyes. The relentless ringing of the fire alarm seemed to pound through his ears.

Then he heard voices to his right and Darcy's voice calling his name.

He and Michigan ran toward the sound, and within moments, the darkness gave way to the dim walls of a long and winding hallway. He felt tile beneath his feet and heard law enforcement sirens in the distance. Vacant doorways lined the wall on either side, with mops, brooms and empty cleaning buckets. A rectangular shaft of light appeared in the distance, and he realized it was the open door leading to the outside.

"Michigan!" he shouted. "Go!"

With a woof, his K-9 partner sped toward the shaft of light. In a moment, the dog had disappeared through the door and outside into the sunshine. Lucas ran after her.

Prayers of thanksgiving filled his heart.

Then a hard, swift blow, with the weight and force of a baseball bat, caught him from behind. He pitched forward. Knees landed hard on his back, pressing him down onto the tile, and he heard the sound of something clattering to the floor. Lucas reared back only to feel the sharp prongs of a stun gun dig into his body, sending paralyzing pain shooting through him.

"You can't leave now, Lucas," a distorted male voice filled his ear. "The game isn't over yet."

SEVEN

Dizziness swept over him as the pounding in his head, the pain of the stun gun and the hazy smoke that had filled his lungs swam together through his senses. He was vaguely aware of the pair of bony knees pressing into his lower back as another jolt of pain shot through his body. He felt thin but strong fingers yanking his useless, floppy arms behind him and tying his hands together with some kind of fabric.

For a moment, time seemed to freeze as he locked his eyes on the open door ahead of him, like a window into the world beyond the burning school. Darcy stood alone at the bottom of the grassy hill on the east side of the building. Faint sirens told him that police cruisers, ambulances and fire trucks were filling the front parking lot. He imagined the STAV Club students who'd been locked inside were running around to the front of the building to check in on their friends and be accounted for with their classmates in the safety roll call.

But Darcy had stayed. Waiting for him.

He saw Michigan bound toward her. Darcy dropped to her knees and wrapped her arms around the golden Lab when the K-9 raced into her arms.

Help me, Darcy!

But she couldn't see him. He couldn't call out to her.

His mind snapped back to reality as he was hit a third time by an even stronger jolt of pain, and he felt rough cloth yanked over his head, blinding his eyes and blocking out the final rays of light.

Darkness filled his gaze, spreading into his mind and tempting him to just pass out and let the pain carry him away into unconsciousness. But he gritted his teeth and prayed for strength. He couldn't let the pain win. He wouldn't let this monster win.

He blew out a long breath and consciously let his body go limp, hoping that if his adversary thought they'd won and he'd passed out, he'd get the chance to regain his strength and fight back. His wrists weren't bound that tightly. He could probably overpower his attacker if it wasn't for the constant, debilitating jolts of pain. Plus, stuns guns had a much shorter range than Tasers. All he needed was to put some distance between himself and those vicious metal prongs.

He was grabbed by the ankles and slowly dragged across the floor, deeper into the bowels of the burning school. The smell of smoke grew thicker.

"I'm sorry you got caught up in this, Lucas." Blaze's voice was every bit as cold and chilling, but something told him that whoever was talking into the voice modulator meant what they were saying. "I hate the fact I'm going to have to kill you. But I don't need you alive for this game, and it'll be an even better one if you're dead. Truth is, I really only planned the game for Ed. But then Darcy had to go stick her nose into things and I couldn't resist toying with her. Especially as Ed's hard to get to right now. But I promise, I'll make your death as quick and painless as I can."

Ironic, considering the cruel infliction of pain they were using to overpower him now. But Lucas knew, with every pain-filled beat of his heart, that the person who now held his life in their hands was going to kill him.

God, please save my life.

He heard the sound of barking echoing down the hallway toward him, as if it was coming from every direction at once. Then came footsteps and Darcy's voice shouting. "Lucas? Lucas! Michigan, where is he?"

"Darcy!" Lucas shouted as loudly as he could, forcing his voice through the hood that covered his face. "Here!"

But even as he shouted her name, doubt and fear filled his mind. Was she running into a trap? Was he about to get her killed?

He heard the ugly, metallic, insect-like sound of the stun gun getting ready to deploy again and braced himself for another burst of voltage.

Instead, Darcy's voice rose in a powerful, warrior-like yell that filled the air. "Let him go!"

It was like everything happened at once. His attacker leaped off him as the distorted voice swore and shouted in what sounded like pain. Michigan snarled and barked in fury. Something wooden crashed in the wall and splintered. He wrenched his hands free, straining his muscles until he felt the fabric tear. Then he yanked the hood off his head to see his K-9 partner standing like a sentry in front of him, growling protectively. In front of her stood Darcy, wielding what looked like the broken remnants of a broom handle, and the indistinct shape of a hooded figure disappeared into the darkness. Beyond that, the smoke and sound of fire moved closer.

"We've got to get out of here." Lucas tried to push up to standing, only to feel his legs buckle weakly beneath him. It was like his entire body was numb and still buzzing in pain.

Darcy spun toward him, threw the broken handle down and reached for him. "It's okay, I've got you."

She slid her shoulder underneath his, wrapped her arm around him and hauled him back up to his feet, even as he tried to find the words to protest. This was ridiculous. He was taller than her—stronger than her—and yet here he was, leaning against her for support as he forced himself to move. Instantly, Michigan moved to flank him on the other side. With one hand, he grabbed ahold of Darcy's; with the other, he gripped the dog's collar tightly. Then together, the three of them half ran, half hobbled out of the burning school.

Soon he felt sunshine beat down against his face. Fresh air filled his lungs, and he looked up to realize they'd made their way outside. Wordlessly, Darcy tried to steer him around to the front of the building, where lights flashed, voices shouted and sirens rose. Instead, he shook his head, gestured up the grassy hill in front of them. Questions filled her dark eyes, but she didn't argue. The trio made their way up the slope until they reached the top. The peak of the hill was so high they could see over the roof of the school from the top of it. Growing up, children from the surrounding area would swarm all over it with toboggans and sleds when school was closed in the winter.

Now the three of them faced the school and sat, with Lucas still in the middle, watching from a safe distance as thick smoke poured from the skylights and flames licked at the auditorium windows. Students huddled around the front of the school as firefighters battled the blaze. Even from this vantage point, he could tell how tightly the scene was under control and how well the response was being coordinated. Silently, he thanked God. Then he forced his hand into his pocket, pulled out his phone, called dispatch, and confirmed that he, Darcy and all the students in the auditorium were out. He ended the call, double-checked he still hadn't gotten a message from his dad and slid his phone back into his pocket, feeling the last ounce of energy drain from his limbs.

He leaned against Darcy, trying to stay upright, and his head fell against the crook of her neck. Michigan lay her head on Lucas's knee. Her large doggy eyes looked up into his face under shaggy golden brows. And suddenly, he realized he was still holding Darcy's hand.

"What happened to you?" Worry flooded Darcy's voice and pooled in her eyes. "Do you need the paramedics? Should I take you to the hospital?"

"No, I'm fine." He shook his head, frustrated at how weak his own voice sounded to his ears. "He just clocked me on the back of the head with something hard and metal. Then kept zapping me with a stun gun to get me to comply." Hearing the gasp slip past Darcy's lips almost hurt more than the physical pain he was in. He silently thanked God that Ed was still in hospital and safe from Blaze's clutches. He felt her hand stroke the back of his head. "Am I bleeding?"

"No."

"Good." He blew out a breath. "I don't want us making a big deal about this, okay? I've taken harder blows, and their aim wasn't that great." If it had been, he'd be dead right now. "And I've been hit with a stun gun before. It's something we go through in basic training. I just need to breathe and wait for the effects to pass."

"It's also protocol to get checked out by paramedics after being hit with a stun gun."

He snorted. "Yeah, you would know that."

She wasn't wrong. He should probably get checked out for injuries and smoke inhalation before leaving the scene. But he'd wait until the staff and students were taken care of first. He looked out over the school to where law enforcement was responding to the crisis. He didn't see any members of the task force, but they'd be arriving soon, if they weren't already there.

"I didn't see the perpetrator," he said. "He—or maybe she—just kind of snuck up on me, smacked me from behind and down I went."

"He or she?" Darcy questioned.

"I honestly couldn't tell if the attacker was male or female," Lucas said and shrugged. "I didn't get a good look at them. I think they had a skinnier frame than me, and used weapons to compensate for the fact they couldn't physically overpower me."

"Well, the Blaze who appeared in my bedroom was definitely a big guy," Darcy said.

"So, there may be two people acting as Blaze," Lucas suggested, "or we have different perceptions of the same person and neither of us are remembering it exactly right. Between the siren, the smoke, the blow to the head and the pain, it's all a jumble."

It was ironic and frustrating. Just hours ago, the team had been lecturing Darcy on not accepting her memories and perceptions as facts. And now he was experiencing the exact same thing.

"All I know for certain is that it was Blaze's voice," Lucas said. "He said he was going to kill me, and I believed him."

He felt Darcy shiver against him. She nestled deeper into his side, until he couldn't tell if she was still the one holding him up or the other way around. Either way, it just felt right to have her there with him.

"The person almost apologized to me," Lucas said. "They said something like, the game had only been planned for my dad and that now the game was for you too. But either way, he didn't need me alive to play it."

Lucas ran the fingers of his free hand over Michigan's head and felt the dog lick his fingers.

"Thank you for coming to rescue me," he said. "I shudder to think where I'd be without you."

"No problem," Darcy said. "You'd have done the same thing for me. In fact, you did yesterday."

Yeah, but it wasn't the same thing.

"When we brief the task force about this, I'd prefer if you left out the part about you having to come to my rescue."

"What?" She stiffened and pulled away.

"Nothing personal." He sat up straight. "I'm new to the team, Darcy, and I'm still trying to prove myself. The last thing I want is for them to think I'm helpless and need to be rescued."

"And how do you think Finnick would've done if he'd been the one smacked over the head and repeatedly zapped by a stun gun?" Darcy asked. She crossed her arms. "Or Caleb? Would they have needed help in the same situation? Or are you the only squishy human member of the team?"

There was a hint of sarcasm to her voice, and now wasn't the time for it. Instead, he held his tongue, stood and started walking toward the front of the school, scanning the crowd of emergency responders for members of his team. She had no idea what it was like to grow up with a father who criticized everything he did and constantly told him that he was never good enough. Or to be the youngest and least experienced member of a team of elite investigators. Not to mention the only cop on the task force who'd actually been rejected when they applied for the Ontario K-9 unit.

She didn't understand that he couldn't shake the gnawing sense in his gut that if he wasn't always at his best, he'd let everybody down. He kept walking and within a breath, he had Michigan by his side and could hear Darcy walking behind him. Yet he didn't let himself turn back. The feeling of her hand seemed to linger in his fingers, and his shoulder still felt warm from having her near. Why had he let himself get that close to her again? Why hadn't he pulled away?

"That wasn't fair," he said after a long moment.

"Oh, really?" Darcy said. "You don't think it's hypocritical to hold yourself to a different standard than you hold other people?"

"I think it's wrong to hold yourself to a lower standard—"

"But not a higher one?"

He turned back. "No, I don't," he said. "I am incredibly thankful you were there for me. You saved my life, and I'll never forget that. And you can tell the team whatever you want. But I'm not going to stand here and argue with you about this. Especially considering that you hold everybody, including yourself, to the highest standard I've ever seen."

She paused for a long moment, and then, to his surprise, she actually laughed.

"Okay!" Her hands rose, palms up. "You're right. You've got me there. It just scared me to see you down on the ground like that, and I don't want you to beat yourself up over it."

He felt a reluctant grin tugging at the edge of his lips. How did this woman get under his skin the way she did? One moment, she was driving him to the edge of frustration and the next she was making him smile?

He turned toward the crowd at the front of the school again. It seemed like everything was in good shape, and already the flames were almost gone, but he doubted the school would be reopening anytime soon. Lucas pulled Michigan's leash from her K-9 vest and looped it around his hand.

Finnick's words flickered in the back of his mind, about how someone was trying to drive Darcy crazy and make her doubt her sanity. Blaze told him that the game he was playing had been originally for Ed and was now for Darcy too. But whatever Blaze was doing, there were hundreds of people now caught up as collateral.

Then suddenly, his eyes alighted on a single figure in the crowd, wearing a white dress shirt, a black tie and somehow…sweatpants.

"Is that who I think it is?" Darcy asked.

"Yeah," Lucas said. And his mind couldn't believe what his eyes were seeing.

There, out of the hospital and in the middle of the emergency response, was the fire chief, his father.

What was he doing here?

Darcy followed as Lucas and Michigan jogged down the side of the hill. His legs still looked a little wobbly, but he definitely seemed a whole lot stronger than when they'd escaped the burning school.

"I don't understand," Lucas said. He sounded flustered, frustrated and more than a little concerned. "All this time, I've been waiting for a call from the hospital. Something to let me know how he was doing and when he'd be released. And now he just shows up?"

He blew out a hard breath.

"I probably owe my stepmother an apology," he added. "When she told me how my dad had shut her out and wouldn't communicate, I didn't really get it. I figured they must've had a fight or that he was going through something. He's always been the kind of guy who was chatty but not open. I figured that if I just moved into the bungalow with him and gave him time, he'd eventually open up. But he was attacked, he was in the hospital, the house where he was living burned down…and he never called his only son? Or gave his doctors permission to fill me in? Or asked me to pick him up?

Instead, he just checks himself out and makes his way here. I don't get it."

"Neither do I," she admitted. They reached the bottom of the hill. "Are you going to go confront him?"

"In my own way and in my own time," Lucas said. "I'm not going to go start yelling at him in public, if that's what you're asking. Thing is, what matters more is getting him to agree to take this Blaze threat seriously and cooperate with the Cold Case Task Force."

He paused. Then he turned back, and his hand brushed her arm.

"Also," he said, "Darcy, please, don't you go confronting him on my behalf. I know you. You've got more fight inside you than anyone I've ever met, and I really like that about you."

She blinked. "Really?"

"Yeah," he said. "I'm really glad I have you in my corner." Something soft moved across his gaze. Then he blinked, and the look vanished. "Anyway, my relationship with Dad has always been complicated. I know your heart is always in the right place, but please, let me handle my dad, my way."

She bit the inside of her cheek and nodded. "Sure."

"Thanks." For a long moment, he held her gaze, as if debating whether or not to say something more. Then he turned and continued walking toward the large-scale response that firefighters and law enforcement were coordinating in front of the building.

Darcy exhaled a long breath and followed, feeling an odd and unfamiliar fluttering within her chest. Why did it feel like, no matter how hard she tried, the past was stubbornly refusing to be ignored?

As they rounded the corner and made their way through the crowd, a tall, blond uniformed policeman jogged toward them. It was Officer Pauly Matthews—husband of Robby's sister, Nicola.

"Lucas!" Pauly called. A wide grin crossed the officer's face.

"Hey, Pauly!" Lucas called back. The two men met in the middle of the crowd and slapped each other on the back. "Is this your scene?"

"This is everybody's scene," Pauly said and laughed. "I think they called every available firefighter, police officer and paramedic on this one. I heard you were the first one on scene and called it in?"

"Something like that," Lucas said.

Pauly waved at Darcy. "Oh, hey, Darce."

"Hey!" She nodded in response.

She'd never known Pauly that well, really only well enough to say hello to in passing. She gathered that he and Lucas had been the kind of childhood friends who got invited to each other's birthday parties but were never close enough for sleepovers. Pauly had dated and married Nicola after Robby had passed away, and as far as she knew, he had never been part of the initial investigation. But she'd always gotten the impression that he was a good guy who loved his wife and his job.

She looked over to see Ed making his way through the crowd toward them as well. The fire chief's white hair was parted sharply to the side and was as perfectly styled as ever. But as Ed turned to say something she couldn't hear to a random firefighter, she couldn't help but notice the long, ugly metallic row of staples that ran down the back of his skull, from where he'd been attacked, and immediately she prayed for his healing.

Had Blaze done that to Ed, as Lucas suspected? Blaze had told Lucas that his "game" had been planned for the fire chief, before he'd then set Darcy in his sights. What kind of danger was Ed in?

Pauly followed her gaze. Then he ran his hand over Michigan's head and turned back to Lucas.

"I hope it's okay," Pauly went on and his smile dimmed, "but I brought your dad here from the hospital. I'd popped over to bring Nicola a coffee because she's been working these crazy long double shifts. And I saw your dad standing there in the lobby."

Lucas blinked. "You brought my father—a man with a recent head wound—to a major fire?"

"He told me that he called you multiple times and you didn't answer," Pauly stammered.

"That's not true," Lucas said and glanced at his phone for confirmation. "I didn't get a single call from him."

"Well, the cell reception isn't the best inside the hospital," Pauly said. "My wife says she often doesn't get my calls. Anyway, Ed asked me to take him to his office. Then when he was in the car with me, I got the call about the fire at the school, and he insisted he grab a fresh shirt from his office and head straight here."

That would explain why his dad was wearing track pants with a uniformed shirt. Presumably he'd only had a spare dress shirt and gym clothes back at the office, and not a fresh pair of slacks.

Lucas looked like he wasn't fully buying Pauly's story. Neither was Darcy.

"How long have you been here?" Lucas asked.

"Oh, only a few minutes," Pauly said.

So, not long enough to be the person who'd attacked Lucas in the school hallway?

Pauly turned to Darcy. "Nicola and I were sorry to hear

there was some kind of commotion at your house in the middle of the night. I hope you're okay."

"There was an intruder on my property," she said, watching her words carefully. "But thankfully everything was fine. I'm guessing that neither of you were working last night?"

Did Pauly—or for thar matter Nicola—have an alibi for last night?

"We were, actually," Pauly said. "There was a major, multi-car accident on the highway and it was all available hands on deck."

She was certain that Lucas and his team would look into verifying that.

Ed was ambling toward them. He met her eye and waved.

"Why, Miss Darcy Lane!" the fire chief's voice boomed. "How are you?"

"Fire Chief Harper," she called back. "It's good to see you."

She made her way toward him, vaguely aware of Lucas thanking Pauly for his help, and Pauly inviting him to bring "yourself, your dog and a date" to a long weekend barbecue he and Nicola were holding.

"It's good to see you too." The fire chief smiled broadly and clasped her on the shoulder as if she were his own daughter. "I heard you got tangled up in that fire situation at my late brother's bungalow. I'm so glad to see you're okay."

"Thanks," she said. "I'm glad to see you're okay too. I heard you took quite the blow."

"Oh, I'm fine," Ed said. "I've got a pretty hard head!"

He laughed boisterously, and while in the past both that and his fatherly gesture would've filled her with warmth, now she could tell that the concerned look in his eyes didn't quite match the smile on his face.

Lucas's words from earlier echoed in her mind. *Dad was*

always charming. Big voice. Bigger personality... But he was never a warm and fuzzy kind of dad.

Before she could say anything more, Ed's gaze swept past her to his son. "Lucas, my boy! I heard you got some kids out of the school. Well done."

"Thanks." Lucas moved over with Michigan by his side as Pauly disappeared back into the crowd. Was it her imagination or did his gaze linger on Ed just a moment too long before turning away? "It was a team effort. I'm sorry that I didn't get your calls about needing me to pick you up from the hospital."

"Pfft." Ed waved his hand noncommittally.

"Speaking of team efforts," Lucas went on, "I know the Cold Case Task Force would really love to talk to you and get your expertise on this whole arson situation..."

"Yeah, yeah, I know." Ed waved both hands now, like he was a traffic cop warning Lucas he was trying to drive the wrong way down a one-way street. "If this is about the whole hoax call, I think you should just move on from that. I'm not going to be able to help with or sit down and talk to your team."

"But, Dad," Lucas began, "you're the one who got Robby to confess. We need your help on this."

Suddenly, something dark flashed through Ed's gaze.

"Son, Harper men don't air their dirty laundry in public, and I haven't got time for this. I've got a scene to manage." His smile broadened but was even less convincing. He patted his son's shoulder. "We'll talk later."

Ed strode off into the crowd, calling out something Darcy couldn't hear to someone she couldn't see. Lucas winced as he watched him go.

"He's hiding something," Lucas said, lowering his voice to prevent being overheard. "I don't know what he's hiding or what, if anything, it has to do with this case. But I'm not going to leave this scene without him." He glanced at his watch. "And you've got to be at work in a little over an hour. I'll get a member of the task force to drive you home to get your car. Unless you want to cancel work and stay here with me. It's clear you're the focus of Blaze's sick game—whatever it is—and I don't want you to get hurt."

His tone was soft, worried and almost tender. Michigan must've sensed it, too, because she nuzzled her snout against Darcy's fingers.

"I'll be fine," Darcy said. She didn't risk looking Lucas in the eyes again, for fear she'd see the same confusing expression she'd seen there before. "I'll be in a giant law enforcement building with cops on every floor. Blaze can't get to me there."

"Okay. I'll place the call."

She was hoping for either Caleb, so she could find out more about the leads he was chasing, or Gemma, so she could quiz her about her efforts to track Blaze digitally.

But instead, the man who arrived at the school to collect her was Jackson, the one member of the team Darcy hadn't met yet. Gemma's brother had a kind smile, a brown beard and a majestic German shepherd K-9 partner named Hudson.

Conversation was light as Jackson drove her back to her house. He explained that he didn't know much about the Blaze investigation. He'd been up north with his fiancée, who ran a bookstore Gemma owned and also had a precocious toddler. He reassured her that Hudson was a top-notch search and rescue dog whose skills at detecting intruders were second to none.

When they reached Darcy's home, Jackson and Hudson searched both the house and the area outside thoroughly but didn't find any trace that somebody else had been there. Jackson waited outside as Darcy got ready for work, then followed her to the dispatch office in his truck. There, they parted ways, and Darcy walked into the 911 call center, greeted her colleagues, logged on and started taking calls.

At first, it was all just the same as any other day.

There were car accidents, thefts, burns and heart attacks. There were callers who were scared and panicked, others who were angry, and still others who just wanted to complain about things that weren't emergencies but that they thought someone should do something about. Her responses were calm, reassuring, direct and succinct. Her fingers moved across the keyboard, summoning and dispatching help. A call would end, she'd breathe a prayer, take a sip of water and move on to the next, letting each one roll off her back as she entrusted those on the other end into the care of God and law enforcement.

Two hours in, she answered yet another call, which began in the same way as all the others.

"911. Police, fire or ambulance?" she greeted.

Then came an odd static crackling down the line, followed by Blaze's distorted voice.

"Hellllo, hoooney," he said. "Are you ready to have a fun and fabulous time?"

EIGHT

The last time she'd heard that voice, she'd been scared. Now she was angry. How dare he terrify those high school students the way he had? How dare he attack Ed and set his bungalow on fire?

How dare he threaten to kill Lucas?

It took all the strength and self-restraint she had to stick to her professional script.

"It's a crime to misuse emergency lines," she responded calmly. "What is your emergency?"

"Listen up, Darcy!" Blaze commanded, voice rising. "Do you feel like a shining star? We all deserve a second chance! Tick tock, tick tock."

The call went dead, and Darcy took a deep breath and thanked God. It was yet another riddle. And this was an easy one. It was the slogan for Shiny's—her favorite second-hand store, the same one she'd recommended to Lucas.

Quickly, she punched in the call, sending a fleet of police officers, paramedics and firefighters to the boutique. Then she fired off a message to the task force alerting them to the threat from Blaze. She sat back in her chair, pulse racing as if she'd just run a marathon.

Let Blaze plot, scheme and play his twisted games.

She was going to beat him, one emergency call at a time.

Her shift continued with the same types of calls she was used to. Yet no matter how hard she tried to focus on whatever call was in front of her, Darcy's mind kept pulling her back to the cell phone she wasn't allowed to have out at work and Blaze's recent call. Had emergency response gotten there in time? Or was he warning of an attack that wasn't happening until sometime in the future? Was the task force any closer to figuring out who this new Blaze copycat even was? She prayed and tried to focus her mind.

An hour before her shift was scheduled to end for the day, she punched the button on the switchboard in front of her to take another call, only to hear the disgusting sound of Blaze laughing at her down the line.

"911," Darcy started. "Police, fire or am…"

But this time the familiar phrase somehow got caught on her tongue and no matter how hard she tried, she couldn't shake it free. This monster was laughing at her. Not just threatening lives. Not just burning down buildings. Not just hurting people and filling them with fear.

He was laughing at her again. Just like he had when he'd broken into her bedroom and stood at the end of her bed the night before. Her hands balled into fists.

"Hellllo, hoooney, are you having fun with our little game?" Blaze asked. "Figured out what we're playing for yet, Darcy Lane? Ready to play another round?"

She glanced at the banks of dispatchers taking calls around her. Then she cupped her hand over her headset microphone and leaned forward.

"Listen here, you demented little cretin," she hissed. "I don't know what game you think you're playing or what right you think you have to destroy other people's lives. We are onto you. We're better than you. And you're not going to win!"

"So spicy!" Blaze said, mockingly. "So sweet. Tick tock, tick tock."

The line went dead. Darcy clenched her jaw and fought the urge to scream.

In that moment, she didn't care who he was, what he wanted, or why he'd somehow decided to make her the focal point of his sick and twisted game.

All that mattered was beating him. She would not—could not—let him win.

She logged the Blaze call in the 911 system, flagging him by name, and then grabbed her cell phone, punched out a message to the Cold Case Task Force letting them know that Blaze had called again, knowing that law enforcement would review the call.

Then she realized she hadn't heard him threaten a target. Or had she missed it?

She ran his words through her mind.

So spicy... So sweet...

Her heart stopped. That hadn't just been a taunt. That was the tagline of the fusion restaurant she'd ordered food from the night before. Quickly, she leaned forward and hit the switchboard, calling in all available units for the restaurant on Main Street. Then she leaned back in her seat, pressed her hand against her heart and stared at the seconds ticking away on her computer's clock. How long had it been since he'd given her that clue? Several seconds? A full minute? Longer? However long it had been, it had been too long for the people needing help.

Fingers shaking, she went back to answering calls. Lights flashed in front of her, waiting to be addressed. Was it her imagination, or was the switchboard busier than usual? Also, worryingly, there seemed to be more people than normal who said they were calling a second or even third time because law enforcement response times were slow.

When her shift finally ended, she removed her headset and logged out of her computer, looking forward to finding out what was the going on in the investigation. Instead, as she pushed her chair back and swiveled around, she looked up to see Simon standing behind her. Concern creased her supervisor's ample brow.

"Miss Lane, can I see you for a moment?"

She blinked. "Is everything okay?"

"Let's talk in my office."

She nodded and followed him down the rows of dispatchers, to his nondescript rectangular office, worry gnawing inside her chest. He closed the door behind them but didn't sit.

"Is everyone at the secondhand shop and fusion restaurant okay?" she asked.

Her supervisor frowned.

"The Blaze call about the secondhand store seems to be a false alarm," he said, "so far. Law enforcement is still onsite, and the bomb squad is taking a very thorough search of the scene." He sighed. "Unfortunately, I can't say the same about the fire at the restaurant. While you were on the call, an explosive device went off in the back kitchen. It caused a grease fire, which spread to the building next door, and firefighters are still struggling to control the blaze. Two people have gone to hospital so far for major burns, as well as half a dozen others for minor burns and smoke inhalation."

Her heart began to sink. "I'm so sorry."

If only she'd solved that riddle faster.

"I've listened to the call," her supervisor went on, "and I regret to inform you that I've decided to suspend you, effective immediately, pending a review of this Blaze situation."

Now her chest ached as if her heart had actually imploded.

"No, you can't do that!" she said. "So far I've been the only one who can solve Blaze's riddles. This is a *regional* call center. None of the other dispatchers would've ever figured out the threat against the high school in Sunset. And how many would know my town well enough to know the slogan of a local eatery? I doubt most of them have ever been to Sunset."

"And that's the problem," Simon said. "I can't have one of my dispatchers tangled up like this. It diverts your attention and makes 911 itself part of this messy situation. Do you know teenagers filmed you when the high school was on fire? You're all over the internet now, with some people calling you a hero, and conspiracy theorists claiming you made the whole thing up just to get famous."

She shook her head. "I'm... I don't know what to say."

"Our job is saving lives," he said. "Hang-up calls were up fifteen percent tonight. I'm guessing because this Blaze character kept hanging up on dispatchers he could tell weren't you. Prank calls are up, too, and I have a responsibility to nip this in the bud before it gets any worse. Whatever game this guy is playing, he's using our 911 call center and local law enforcement as part of it, and I can't let that happen."

"But if I'm not here, there will be no one to solve his riddles," Darcy said.

"Possibly," her supervisor said, "or, more likely, when it's announced you've been suspended and he finds out you're not working, he'll stop calling 911 looking for you."

"You can't do this!" Couldn't he see that? "I know I let that one call get out of hand, and I'm sorry. But if you suspend me now, you're risking people's lives."

"Or I'm saving them," he said. "I'm sorry, Miss Lane, but the decision has already been made."

Her mind was in a haze as she left his office and walked down the stairs to her car. She got in the driver's seat and sat there for a long moment, too frozen by what had just happened to even know what to do next. Then she started the car and began to drive. She left the highway, turning down one rural road after another, moving deeper and deeper into the woods. Her hands were shaking as she gripped the steering wheel. A deep pink sunset spread across the fields and trees ahead of her. An odd smell that made her think of swimming pools and locker rooms seemed to float on the air.

Then she heard something click from behind her. She gasped, but there was nothing there but an empty back seat, just the same as she'd left it.

The outskirts of Sunset lay ahead of her. She slipped her phone into the hands-free mount on her dashboard and dialed Lucas.

A second later, his comforting voice filled her car. "Hey, Darce! I saw there were two Blaze 911 calls at work today?"

"Yeah." Her voice came out watery and weak. Thick tears filled her eyes. She blinked hard to stop them from falling.

"You all right?" he said. "You sound upset. I'm by the lake with Michigan right now. Unbelievably, Dad refused to go back to the farmhouse with me and checked himself into a motel near the fire hall. So I decided to take Michigan for a run to let off some steam. But I'll be home in a bit. Then we can sit down and talk about it and also how we're going to arrange your protection detail for tonight."

That was barely five minutes' drive from where she was now. She opened her mouth to say she could meet him at the park, only for her voice to come out as a sudden, uncontrollable sob. The tears she'd managed to fight off so far, now burst unexpectedly from her eyes and ran down her cheeks.

"Hey!" Concern moved through Lucas's voice. "Are you okay? Where are you? I'm on my way to you now."

"No, it's okay," she managed, tears filling her voice. "I'll make my way to you. I'm not on the main road."

The road slowed steeply in front of her. She pressed down on the brake, expecting the car to slow. Instead, the pedal fell floppy and useless beneath her foot. In an instant, her tears turned to terror.

"I think someone messed with my brakes!" she let out. "I can't stop!"

She could hear Lucas shouting on the other end of the line. But his words were swallowed up by the sound of something rumbling behind her. Panicked, she glanced up in her rearview mirror, just in time to see the back seat of her car go up in flames.

"My car's on fire!" Darcy's terrified voice echoed down the phone, sending waves of fear crashing over Lucas's heart. He ran across the top of the cliff, with Michigan by his side, and back toward the trail they'd hiked up, for the moment not even knowing where he was going.

Lord, help me find her. Help me save her!

"Your car engine's on fire?"

"No, my back seat!" she yelled. "The fire is in the car with me!"

Panic pounded through his veins. He couldn't believe what he was hearing. "Can you jump out?"

"I can't open the door!" she yelled. "I'm locked in. I can't stop! I can't even slow down!"

"I'll find you! Tell me what road you're on—"

The phone went dead as the call dropped. He called dispatch immediately to report that a vehicle with her make, model and license plate was somewhere on a rural road near

Lake Simcoe with faulty brakes and a fire in the back seat. He ended that call, too, and finally stopped running. Lucas stood there with his feet in the soft earth and his faithful K-9 partner whimpering by his side. Trees waved in the evening breeze around him. A sunset spread over the still waters of Lake Simcoe beneath him. His heart raced so hard he could feel it beating inside his throat, choking his breath from his lungs.

He was helpless. Darcy was out there somewhere, in danger for her life. And he had no way to find her. No way to help her.

Lucas dropped to his knees in the dirt.

"Lord, be with Darcy right now. Help her. Save her." His head fell into his hands. "I feel like I just got her back. And I can't bear the thought of losing her again."

Then he heard the sound of Michigan sniffing the air and her paws dancing on the soft ground. His eyes snapped open. His partner was detecting something.

"You can smell it, can't you?" he asked, hope rising in his chest. "You can smell the fire?"

He stood. "Show me."

Michigan began to bark. Her voice was loud, urgent and triumphant. Then she began to run. Lucas sped after her, pushing his body through the brush and following his partner as together they cut a new and unknown path through the forest.

The trees parted, and cliffside lay in front of them with the blue-black waters of Lake Simcoe spreading out beneath. There was nowhere left to run.

Then he saw Darcy's car flying down a narrow rural road beneath him like a flaming comet piercing the sky. Thick black smoke engulfed the inside of the small car so completely he couldn't even see her. His breath froze. The road disappeared in front of her tires. Her car shot out over the rocks. For a moment, it caught air, before it plunged nose first into the lake and sank beneath its inky blue depths.

He grabbed a heavy rock and kicked off his shoes.

"Michigan! Jump!"

He took a deep breath and dove off the side of the cliff, his arms and legs locking tight to his side as he fell through the air. His body cut cleanly through the water. He felt Michigan land beside him and follow him deeper into the lake, but Lucas didn't look back. Instead, he swam straight down into the murky water, scanning for her. For a moment, nothing but dark water filled his eyes.

Then he saw the eerie orange glow of Darcy's car sinking in the depths beneath him.

He swam for it, pushing his body as fast as he could through the water. As he drew close, he could see Darcy's panicked face inside the vehicle, her skin pale and eyes wide, as she struggled with the door, battling to break herself free.

He waved at her to move back, then bashed the rock as hard as he could into the windshield, over and over again, until he could see a spiderweb of cracks beginning to spread across the glass. His lungs ached for air. But he didn't let himself stop. He wouldn't go back to the surface without her, not even to catch his breath.

The windshield finally gave way, caving in on itself in a folding maze of shattered glass. He lunged through, grabbed ahold of Darcy's hand and yanked her free as water poured into the vehicle.

He swam toward the surface, half guiding, half pulling Darcy along with him. Then she pulled away, and he let her hand go as, side by side, they pressed their way through the water. Together they broke through and gasped. Fresh air filled their lungs. Michigan met them as they surfaced. In an instant, Michigan swam to Darcy's side and nudged her snout underneath her arm.

"She's offering to help carry you to shore," he said.

Darcy nodded and gasped a painful-sounding breath. Then she grabbed ahold of Michigan's K-9 vest, draped her arm and shoulder over the golden Lab, and the three of them swam for dry land. He felt thick mud and slick rock beneath his stockinged feet. They climbed up onto the shore and collapsed on the ground.

"Thank you, Lord," Darcy whispered.

"Amen," he echoed.

Then Lucas pulled himself up, sat cross-legged on the ground and looked out over the water, where her burning car lay buried. Darcy collapsed into his side. He wrapped his arm around her, and her head fell on his shoulder, in the same way he'd leaned against her when she'd helped him out of the burning school earlier. Michigan lay on the ground in front of their feet, panting. Lucas fished his phone from his pocket, thanked God that the waterproof case had worked and called dispatch to fill them in. He followed up with a group text message to the cold case team, with his exact GPS coordinates so they could find the right road. Then he let the phone drop and felt the exhaustion of what had just happened finally hit his body.

"I can't believe your dad would rather check into a hotel instead of stay at the farmhouse with you," Darcy said. It wasn't what he'd expected her to begin with. But that was Darcy.

"Neither can I." He shrugged. Then he turned toward her. "Are you okay?"

His voice sounded oddly gruff in his throat.

"Yeah," Darcy said. She nodded and he felt her head brush against his cheek. "I mean, no. Everything is terrifying and bad. My laptop, my phone and my purse are now all at the bottom of Lake Simcoe. I've been attacked, someone broke into my home, I've lost my car and I haven't even filled you in about work yet."

He remembered how she'd been crying on the phone before she realized someone had tampered with her car. "Do you want to talk about it?"

"In a moment." Darcy turned toward him, and his hand slid to the back of her neck. "Right now, I'm just going to take a breath, center myself first, and be thankful we're both alive and safe. Well, all three of us, counting Michigan."

A smile brushed her delicate lips, which somehow seemed to send golden light dancing in the depths of his heart. Strands of wet hair clung to the side of her cheeks. He reached up with his other hand and tucked them back behind her ear. His fingers lingered on her face.

"I know this might sound silly..." she went on, and her chin rose. She was so close to him now that he could feel her breath brush along his jaw. "But I'm still holding on to the faith that we're going to beat this new Blaze copycat and that everything is going to be okay. I'm not going to give up hope. I'm not going to let fear and despair win. That's what Blaze wants. And we're not going to let him get the best of us. You were the best friend I've ever had, and I always felt as long as you and I were together, nothing could defeat us."

"I always felt that way about you too," he said, "and I haven't given up hope either."

He leaned forward. His nose brushed against Darcy's.

And then Lucas kissed her.

NINE

The kiss was tentative at first. Lucas had always remembered the kiss that he and Darcy had shared as teenagers as being overwhelming, emotional and impulsive—the equivalent to hurling himself off the edge of a cliff and falling down into the ocean below.

But this kiss was different. It was gentle—tender and sweet—as if both of them were testing the waters and trying to figure out how deep they really went. Slowly, her arms slid around his neck, and his wrapped around her back. Then their kiss ended. But still they stayed there, with their foreheads gently resting against each other's, breathing each other in.

"I missed you," he said, finally. "Like, a lot."

"I missed you too," she said. "I wish you'd called or emailed, or even texted me."

"You told me not to."

She sat back, pulling her arms away from him. In the dying light, he watched as genuine confusion filled her eyes. "No, I didn't."

"Yeah, you did." He sat back too. As much as he didn't want to reopen that whole can of worms from their past, he also needed her to know why he'd stayed away. "The morning after we kissed, I called you. I told you that I was sorry, and I said that the kiss had been a mistake."

"I remember," Darcy said, stiffly. She stood, and her arms crossed tightly across her chest. He stood, too, and Michigan scrambled to her feet as well. "You told me that you didn't like me that way and made me feel like an idiot for saying I liked you."

Had he said that? If so, he didn't remember.

"I thought I said that I really cared about you but that I wanted to just focus on being friends," Lucas said. Was that the same thing? In his mind, there'd been some nuance there, but maybe it hadn't come across that way. "I also pointed out that I was leaving for British Columbia in the morning and we could talk in person when I got back in a few months. You got all upset, started calling me names, told me you hated me and that you never wanted to hear from me or see my stupid face ever again."

Darcy stepped back.

"I don't remember that," she said. "I mean, I do definitely remember that conversation and you saying something like that. But you're making it sound like you were being really nice and I was being irrational and mean." Her head was shaking. "This was a mistake."

What was? The kiss? Talking about the past? Calling him for help with Blaze?

All of the above?

He felt defeated. "Yeah, you're probably right," he said.

At least as far as the first two things were concerned. He heard the sound of tires crunching on the dirt road and looked up to see both Finnick's and Jackson's trucks coming down the road. He was thankful for the interruption. Michigan woofed in greeting and wagged her tail. He started toward them, turning his back on the lips he'd just foolishly kissed and the conversation that was starting to spin out of control.

The last thing he wanted, or needed, was for his new colleagues in the Cold Case Task Force to see him all flustered and thrown from a kiss with a witness that he never should've let happen.

The trucks stopped, doors opened, and Michigan barked joyfully as Nippy and Hudson leaped out of their respective vehicles. Michigan glanced at Lucas for permission to join then.

"Go on, Michi," he told the K-9. The golden Lab woofed in thanks and bounded through the scrub toward them. The three dogs greeted each other joyously.

The four humans made their way across the ground toward each other with far grimmer and more solemn faces and stood in a huddle.

"Are you okay?" Finnick asked Darcy.

"I'm safe, alive and well," Darcy said. "And sometimes that's the best we can hope for."

"Agreed," Finnick said. "Unfortunately, it might be a while before anyone comes to get your car out of the lake."

"Because the call has been deemed low priority," Darcy supplied, "as no one is in imminent danger, right?"

"That's it exactly," Finnick said. "Also law enforcement is really stretched thin right now due to the high school fire, followed by the two Blaze calls."

"Yeah, dispatch is really overloaded right now too," Darcy said. She frowned and Lucas remembered she'd implied something not great had happened at work today. "Is the restaurant fire out?"

"No, but it's under control and no longer in danger of spreading," Jackson said. "I just came from there. No fatalities. No serious injuries but a few moderate ones, including two bad burns."

Lucas prayed silently for the victims of the fire and that Blaze would be caught soon. A silence fell around the group, and he suspected the others were doing the same.

"Thankfully, there still seems to be no fire or explosive devices at the secondhand store," Jackson added.

Darcy took a deep breath and rolled her shoulders back.

"I've been temporarily suspended from my job at the 911 call center," she said, "pending a review of the Blaze situation."

"Oh, Darce, I'm so sorry," Lucas murmured. His hands flinched to reach for her, comfort her, but he stopped and held himself back.

"My supervisor, Simon Phillips, said there'd been a major spike in prank calls today," she went on, and he wasn't sure if she'd heard him. "Seems Blaze might've just kept calling and hanging up over and over again until he got me. Also, apparently high school students have been posting video clips online of me helping evacuate the auditorium."

"You have become a 'meme,'" Jackson confirmed, putting air quotation marks around the word.

"My supervisor said that the whole thing with Blaze has diverted my attention from my job," Darcy continued, "and is impacting the whole center. He thinks that maybe if word gets around that I'm not there, Blaze will stop calling 911 incessantly And, while these aren't his exact words, he said Blaze is making 911 itself a part of his game."

"Can't argue with that," Finnick said. "Blaze has turned 911 itself—and frankly all of local law enforcement—into game pieces."

"The question is, how this copycat knew how to play first responders," Jackson said. "Because I've reviewed the write-up Gemma did on the original Blaze. And all I see in Robby Lamb is a really smart kid, pulling deadly and highly dangerous, but still kid-level, pranks. Whatever's going on here, this copycat has taken it to a whole new level. Five major callouts in a little over twenty-four hours, all from untraceable numbers and two of which were pranks."

Darcy glanced sharply from Finnick to Jackson to Lucas and back, as if she couldn't believe that none of them were leaping to her defense but instead agreeing with her supervisor.

"But none of this is my fault," Darcy said. "I mean, I did lose my temper and went off script with the final Blaze call. But I don't deserve to be suspended."

Lucas didn't know what to say to that, and his colleagues didn't speak either. The sun set deeper into the lake. A colder breeze moved through the air and permeated his soaked clothes, which still stuck to him like badly packaged food wrap. Finally, he was the one who broke the awkward silence. "Obviously, nobody thinks you deserve to be threatened, stalked and harassed, Darcy. But Jackson's right. This new Blaze has taken things to a whole new level, involving large-scale law enforcement response. Emergency-response time is down, and that's incredibly dangerous. Dispatch has got to consider the impact having you there is going to have on 911's ability to respond to genuine emergencies."

Darcy's jaw rolled slowly as if she was being forced to digest a very bitter pill she didn't much want to swallow. "And of course you guys know that apparently some internet conspiracies say I made the whole thing up just to get famous?"

"I do," Finnick admitted. "Gemma's been looking into it. For what it's worth, she said naturally occurring internet traction doesn't normally happen so fast, so it's possible Blaze is behind that too."

"Of course Blaze is behind it." Darcy sighed. Then, suddenly, it was like a thought had just dawned behind her eyes. Suspicion filled her face. "Hang on, I haven't seen Caleb since yesterday, and I still don't know if Gemma has figured out where Blaze texted me from. Are you guys investigating me?"

"Yeah," Finnick said, quickly and without a flicker of regret or embarrassment. "Gemma tracked Blaze's text to a phone registered in your name. Caleb is investigating an anonymous call that came into Crime Stoppers before dawn this morning, saying that you invented Blaze—both then and now. You're by no means the only person we've been investigating. So far we've confirmed the security guard's family had no involvement in this. But we're still seeking confirmation of Pauly's work schedule to verify he has an alibi every time a Blaze attack occurred. I told you from the beginning that we'd look into everything, and that includes you. Because you never know where a lead is going to take you."

"Even if Blaze is planting those leads?" Darcy challenged.

"*Especially* if Blaze is planting those leads," Finnick said, crossing his arms.

Darcy turned to Lucas. He wanted to tell her that he had no idea what specific leads Caleb and Gemma had been chasing. But at the end of the day it didn't matter, because his team had every right to look into every possible angle, including Darcy.

For a brief moment, fire flashed through her eyes, and Lucas thought she was about to start arguing with his team, right there on the muddy ground beside the lake.

Then she closed her eyes, what looked like a silent prayer moved on her lips and as he watched, peace, or at least calm, washed over her features.

She opened her eyes and turned to Finnick.

"I want to go home," she said, "to my house. I appreciate Lucas letting me stay at the farmhouse last night, but I'd rather be in my own place and surrounded by my own stuff. But my car is in the lake, and I don't know if I need to stay to wait for the emergency vehicles to get here."

"It's okay," Finnick said, and there was a softness to his boss's tone. "Nippy and I will take you home, make sure everything's safe and secure and that you're under surveillance all night. Tomorrow, we'll check in and see where we're at." Then he glanced at Lucas. "We'll also have surveillance on the motel Ed is staying at. I was sorry to hear he decided not to go home with you."

Darcy wrapped her arms around herself and suddenly looked exhausted. She turned to Lucas, but even though her words were directed toward him, he realized she wasn't really looking at him. "Thanks again for helping me out of that car. I'd be dead at the bottom of the lake without you."

He opened his mouth but no words came out, and before he could find any, she turned and started for Finnick's truck. The trio of dogs followed along, flanking her as if to reassure her that she was part of their pack. She stopped to pat all three, giving them all equal attention, before climbing up into the truck.

Help me, Lord. Everything is a mess, and I want to comfort and help her, but I don't know what to say.

She climbed into the passenger seat and reached over to close the door.

"Darce!" he called.

She turned toward him and her dark eyes met his.

"I'm sorry about everything," he said, thankful that his colleagues wouldn't know everything he was referring to. "I know the whole situation feels pretty messy right now. Maybe even hopeless. But, like I told you before, you've got more fight inside you than anyone I've ever met. And like you told me, you are not going to let Blaze defeat you. Whoever this new copycat is, and whatever he wants, he is not going to win. Because you're stronger than him. I promise you that."

Tears glistened in Darcy's eyes. He wanted to run across the ground and gather her up in a hug. Instead, he stood back beside Jackson and watched as she left in Finnick's truck. Michigan and Hudson ran back to join their human partners, and his boss's vehicle disappeared from view.

"So, where are your shoes?" Jackson asked.

Lucas looked down at his muddy socks. "Top of the cliff. I kicked them off when I dove in after her."

He gestured in the direction he'd left them. Jackson nodded, and together the two K-9 officers slowly made their way up the slope while their partners woofed and galloped past them.

"Why didn't you ask me sooner?" Lucas wondered.

"Because Finnick didn't ask," Jackson said, "and I know he noticed. Finnick notices everything." He chuckled. "I'm a good enough cop to know there's some complicated history between you and Darcy. But you should know that Finnick has the kind of laser focus to pinpoint exactly what it is. You can't hide anything from him. Trust me, I've tried and it did not go well."

He laughed a little as if recalling a memory. Lucas continued to pick his way over the rocky ground.

"Do you think he could tell that I kissed her and regret it?" Lucas asked.

To his surprise, Jackson guffawed loudly and slapped him on the shoulder.

"Yeah, I'm pretty sure he could, if that's what you did," Jackson said. "And trust me, he does not like discovering that one of his officers let interpersonal foolishness compromise a case. So my advice is to talk to him right away, be open about it and listen seriously to any advice he gives."

Lucas sighed. And prayed that he wouldn't get booted off the team.

Lucas is definitely not my favorite person right now, Darcy thought as Finnick drove her home through the trees. In fact, she could feel a whole mess of complicated, confusing and upsetting feelings swirling around inside her, making her unsure if she was about to cry or yell. But on the other hand, it had been really good to hear Lucas remind her that she was not going down without a fight.

Lucas Harper might be the most infuriating man she'd ever met. And kissing him again after he'd rescued her might've been the biggest mistake she'd made since the last time she'd kissed him.

But he was right. She'd never been a particularly big or physically strong person. Most years in school, she'd either been *the* shortest or *one* of the shortest kids in class. But there'd always been this spark—a drive—within her to do everything in her power to fight for truth, goodness, justice and faith. In fact, she'd been so used to feeling that way that it took her a long time to realize that not everybody was wired like she was.

She silently asked God to guide her and show her how to win this fight. Her mind began to spin in a furious brainstorm of all the different steps she could take and things she could do, yet her attempts to strategize kept getting distracted. Then a still and soft voice in the back of her mind whispered to her: *Be gentle and kind.*

Her eyes snapped open. Now where had that thought come from? She stared at the darkness outside as she viscerally pushed back against it. Gentle and kind? Well, she liked to think she was always kind. As for being gentle, there was no place for gentleness in a fight.

When she got home, Darcy waited by her front door while Finnick and Nippy searched her house and declared it safe. Finnick told her he and Nippy would hang out in his truck for a while—assuring her he had some work to do and that he loved hanging out in his truck. He'd enjoy the quiet away from his fiancée and their soon-to-be-adopted baby. Jackson and Hudson, he added, would come take his place in a bit, and they'd camp overnight outside her home. He reassured her that he and the cold case team were pouring all their resources into finding and stopping Blaze and that they would continue to do so until he was brought to justice. She thanked him.

But her attention had already been pulled so far into her own plans that the inspector might as well have been explaining the details of an investigation that didn't involve her. If the Cold Case Task Force was spending even two seconds looking into her, then clearly they weren't putting their full attention into the right things. And that was okay, because by the time the sun set, and she was tossing and turning that night in her bed, she'd come up with a pretty solid list of how she was going to tackle things on her own the next day.

Thanks to having a landline, she was able to cancel her debit and credit cards and order replacements for everything she'd lost. Then she called the town librarian at home and booked the research room in the basement of the library for the following morning, along with borrowing a library laptop and cell phone.

Most importantly, she had her target list of people she was going to investigate.

Top of the list was Corporal Austin Dillon. Not that she

had any reason to link him to Blaze, except for the fact that he'd always been a mean and nasty jerk, who'd hidden it well behind a charming smile. He'd doubted her truth from the beginning of this whole copycat situation, and he had the ability and access to pull off something of this scale.

Next came her supervisor, Simon Phillips. True, he'd always seemed like a nice guy, or at least a mild and boring one. But he definitely fit the description of being both a tall man, like the Blaze who'd broken into her house, and someone with a bony frame, like the person who'd attacked Lucas. Plus, there was still the unexplained fact that Lucas's father had dismissed the original 911 call as a hoax. Was that Simon's doing?

Ed was on the list too. He'd done a laundry list of unexplained and dodgy things lately. Maybe he was being blackmailed by this new Blaze copycat. Maybe he'd been blackmailed by the original Blaze and it had never been Robby Lamb—not that it seemed likely at all. Despite the online theories, she was certain Robby was dead. And as it had been pointed out earlier, the Blaze of the past struck her as a kid, executing teen-level pranks. This new offender was different, much more sophisticated.

Theories were rampaging through her mind now. Gemma had asked what the pattern was in the targets Robby had chosen to burn down. Maybe if Darcy went over all his old targets, she'd find a pattern there. The school library was gone, but the town's archives in the public library would have school yearbooks, flyers, notices, posters for old play productions and even local newspapers that wouldn't be online. She could research the history of his past targets and the new ones.

Then there were Robby's family members who still lived in Sunset. Pauly was a cop and Nicola was a paramedic. Both had probably been all over the crime scenes, not to mention having the skills and contacts needed to pull this off. Could Pauly be the Blaze who'd broken into her bedroom and Nicola the Blaze who'd attacked her and Lucas? It was definitely possible, considering both her build and strength as a paramedic. Robby's mother, Bea, was her son's strongest defender and had been fighting tirelessly to clear Robby's name. But Bea didn't have the physical strength to have attacked either her or Lucas.

The only evidence that Caleb had outside Darcy's home the night of the attack were a few unexplained and circular marks. But maybe Caleb himself wasn't trustworthy. For that matter, she'd see what she could find out about the members of the Cold Case Task Force, too, considering they were happily researching her. For all she knew, one of them was involved. It would definitely explain why the investigation was going nowhere and getting tangled up in knots. The task force had also cleared the family of Jim Scott—the security guard who'd died in the warehouse fire. Robby Lamb's only homicide victim. Maybe they'd been wrong in that too.

She slept fitfully, drifting in and out of consciousness. Her eyes kept turning to the bright, red electronic numbers on her clock as they ticked forward, and she willed morning to come. Four words kept running through her mind.

Be gentle and kind.

But was there actually a way to combat Blaze while also being gentle and kind?

She realized that she'd said something like that to Lucas after Blaze had broken into her house.

You have this way of being strong that's also gentle and kind.

Unbidden, his face filled her mind. She remembered how it had been to be in his arms, the feeling of his hand brushing the back of her neck, and the look that had filled his green eyes just before their lips met in a kiss. But that had been followed by a sudden sharp pain in her gut when he'd told her that she'd explicitly said she never wanted to hear his voice or see his face again. In which case, he'd have actually been respecting *her* wishes by not reaching out. Right? But if she'd said that—and despite her protests, she had to assume she had—he'd known she didn't mean it, right?

A loud and jarring ringing filled her ears. She sat up to realize it was seven thirty in the morning and sunshine was already seeping in through the window. Morning had come. It was time to push Lucas out of her mind and focus on catching the criminal who'd been hunting her.

She got ready for the day, then made a pot of coffee and poured it into two travel mugs—one for her and one for whichever member of the Cold Case Task Force she'd find when she opened her front door.

It turned out to be Jackson, just as Finnick had predicted. She found him inside the covered back cab of his pickup truck, which seemed to have been converted into a cross between a mobile trailer and makeshift tent. Through the windshield, she could see that he was awake and reading a crime novel that had a large turquoise sticker for Clearwater Bookstore on its cover. Hudson was stretched out, his large, shaggy form taking up a good two-thirds of the available space. But even though the German shepherd's eyes were closed, the way his nose twitched and ears perked as she approached let her know that the elite Search and Rescue K-9 dog hadn't dropped his guard for moment.

She knocked on the driver's-side window.

"Good morning!" Jackson smiled easily as he climbed into the front seat, opened the driver's-side door and reached for the coffee she offered him. "Thank you kindly. Lucas has invited us both over to his farmhouse for eggs and pancakes whenever you're ready."

Her stomach grumbled. She ignored it. She didn't need comfort food right now. Or the emotional comfort of seeing Lucas's face.

What she needed were answers.

"Thanks," she said. "But I've booked private use of the research room in the basement of the town library, and I hoped you could drive me over...as soon as possible."

His smile dimmed slightly, as if his brain was taking a moment to process what she was saying.

She smiled even wider as if to compensate. "I've even got a loaner cell phone and laptop waiting for me, along with a whole list of local things I want to research. Blaze keeps using very specific local references in his riddles. There might be something, written on a physical flyer or piece of paper, that holds the key to something we need to know."

"Huh," Jackson said. "I'm impressed. Lucas did warn you were a bit of a live wire. Have you ever considered a career as a police officer?"

"Thanks." Darcy felt herself flush at the unexpected compliment. Lucas had said that about her? "I appreciate it, but I feel pretty sure my life's calling is as a 911 dispatcher, and I can't wait to get back to it."

"Hop in," he said and chuckled. She went around to the passenger door, got in and buckled up. "You remind me of my sister. Gemma is unbelievably stubborn and independent too. She's a private detective, despite the fact we've all told her that she should join the force. She's so skeptical of the police, the fact I went into law enforcement caused a rift between us for ages, but we're good now. I can see why Finnick decided to take you on. He might be a bit of a grump, but he likes spunk."

Darcy smiled. They drove into town, arrived at the library ten minutes before it opened and grabbed bagels at the café across the street.

"I need to take Hudson for a walk," Jackson said, "and check in with the team. Do you want me to arrange to have someone posted outside the library?"

"No, thanks," Darcy said. "They've got cameras in the main areas, and I won't leave without checking in with the team first."

Hopefully with a whole lot of new and helpful information.

She thanked Jackson sincerely, patted Hudson goodbye, and then walked into the library with her jaw set and her head held high, determined not to walk back through the door again without some answers.

The Sunset town library was small but beautiful. Colorful message boards up front were filled with flyers for town groups, clubs and school events along with children's art. Long wooden shelves weaved a cozy labyrinth of books around a semicircular librarian's desk. Wide steps to the right led upstairs to a children's area lined with bright and cheerful cutouts of animals, sea creatures and mythical beasts.

Darcy picked up her borrowed laptop and cell phone from the front desk, gave the librarian a very long written list of the archive boxes she wanted, and then turned left and walked down the narrow stairs to the research room. The joyful colors gave way to bland walls that were somehow neither beige nor gray, but some unimpressive shade in between. An ugly gray metal door to the right of the stairs hid a small elevator. The basement room was small and rectangular, with a plain white conference table, four metal chairs and a single tiny glass window set high above her head. But the laptop worked, and there were no distractions.

Especially not a handsome and confusing one with amazing green eyes.

She pulled a spiral notebook out of her bag and began to work.

But despite her plan to methodically tackle each suspect on her list one by one, instead she found her mind hopping around from topic to topic, pulling at new threads as she discovered them and getting up periodically to check the hallway outside the door.

The number of boxes she'd requested the librarians pull from the archives was close to fifty, and that included their meticulous filing of the physical editions of the local paper, which had ads for businesses and notices that never made it onto the online version, along with every approved flyer and piece of artwork they'd ever displayed when they were taken down and changed over. Due to the volume, library staff would be pulling a few at a time during the day, and bring them down in the small elevator, rather than trying to grab them all at once.

She started by checking online news for any arrest reports and unflattering news involving every person on her list. But quickly, she moved on to any news reference at all that she could find. Then she moved on to available social media while flipping through the physical contents of the boxes. It was like falling down a deep rabbit hole.

Bit by bit, she filled the notepad full of interesting but potentially unrelated facts. She couldn't find anything on the dates of the Blaze copycat attacks or why he'd resurface now. The only special date she could see on the calendar was the May long weekend, and that fell on different days every year. It wasn't Robby Lamb's birthday, the anniversary of his death or the first fire, or some other significant date for him or his family, that she could find. So if there was a reason why the copycat had struck now, it wasn't any of those.

Austin's career record seemed spotless, although according to the local paper he had been sued once for not paying his contractor. Simon had won a model train competition once and interestingly also hosted a charity auction event at the secondhand store. Ed's recent driving accident had been much worse than she'd realized, with the print version of the newspaper showing black-and-white photos of his demolished truck wrapped around a tree on a small and unpaved rural road deep in the countryside. The crash had occurred in the middle of nowhere, with no witnesses. And there were no such photos in the website version of the paper, but an extensive search through archived versions showed the photos had once been online, too, but then removed. Maybe Ed had complained. The weekly paper only printed a few hundred physical copies these days for the town archives and local businesses. Most people read it online. Maybe someone had reached out to Ed for comment before it was distributed and he talked them into pulling it.

The restaurant that Robby's Blaze had destroyed had once been a private family place, beloved by children before it was bought out by a corporate chain with a policy of banning teenagers who didn't come in with an adult. The empty warehouse where security guard Jim Scott had died had been a former children's arcade, music store and indoor miniature golf site before being bought by a developer. In fact, the biggest pattern she could see emerging in her tapestry was the story of Sunset itself. When she was young, it was full of small businesses, mom-and-pop shops, and the kind of houses people could actually afford. But then, piece by piece, the small town had transformed into something more expensive and less friendly. The forest bike trails kids rode on were demolished for new expensive town houses. The Honey Bee Drive-In, which teenagers swarmed to en masse over the May long weekend for its annual opening night— when popcorn was free—had since been bought by a major corporate chain. She gazed at a bright yellow flyer for one of the last events before the change had been made. A cartoon bee mascot in dark sunglasses smiled up at her. The figure who'd always welcomed them all to events on the big screen. She even found a flyer for the zoning protest Robby had invited her to the year before he died. He'd wanted to fight what was happening to his town. Had he taken drastic measures to do that?

A knock on the door interrupted her train of thought. Another stack of boxes had arrived. She stood, stretched, crossed the floor and reached for the door handle.

It didn't move. She tried again, harder. It rattled slightly but wouldn't budge.

She knocked on the door. "Hello? Can somebody come open the door?"

"Hellllo, hoooney." Suddenly, Blaze's cruel voice sounded from behind her, inside the reference room, seeming to come from everywhere at once. "Ready to play the final round, Darcy? It starts tonight when the sun goes down."

It sounded like he was coming from under the table. Then there was a bang. Thick smoke filled the room, and bright orange flames flashed before her eyes. She was trapped in the basement with Blaze—and there was no means of escape.

TEN

"Lucas! I'm so glad you could make it to our little party!" Nicola's voice floated above the happy chatter of the long-weekend backyard barbecue. He glanced up to see Nicola moving through the crowd of people gathering around the sun-soaked grass in a long, flowy top and leggings. Her arms spread wide in greeting. "I heard from Pauly that you brought a date!"

"Hi, Nicola, meet Gemma." Lucas arranged his face into a cheerful smile and turned to the pretty brunette in the sundress beside him. "Gemma, meet Nicola."

It had been Finnick's idea to send Gemma along with Lucas to the barbecue. It had been decided in a team meeting earlier that morning. When Jackson had called Lucas to let him know that Darcy had gone straight to the library, he didn't know whether to be disappointed or relieved, and he just ended up feeling a big old dose of both. But his logical cop side could see how bringing Gemma to the barbecue was far less complicated. They could gather intel and keep their ears open for new leads.

The team meeting had been quick, efficient and lacking in results. The good news was that Caleb's investigation into the anonymous tips against Darcy had all turned out to be false, and Gemma hadn't been able to confirm that Darcy had purchased Blaze's burner phone, which meant it couldn't have been someone using her name to buy it. Caleb reported that Ed had walked to work at the fire house in the morning. Neither Ed nor Darcy had any untoward visitors lurking anywhere near where they slept during the night.

The barbecue was full of other responders, including Austin Dillon, and would also give Lucas the opportunity to talk to Nicola about Robby.

And that was how Lucas, his private eye coworker and K-9 partner Michigan ended up standing in Nicola and Pauly's lush backyard, mingling with cops, doctors, paramedics and firefighters from across the area while dressed in his best button-down shirt, with Michigan sporting a bright yellow bow on her collar.

"You have a beautiful home!" Gemma stepped forward and reached for Nicola's hands, clasping them in hers. Her blue eyes sparkled as she glanced around the vegetable garden and flower beds. "I can't believe there's an oasis like this so close to the middle of town. Thank you so much for including me!"

"Not a problem," Nicola said. The two women squeezed hands like long-lost friends and let go. "It's a pleasure to have you. I have to admit, I was really surprised when I heard Lucas called me this morning and confirmed he could bring a date. I had no idea he was seeing someone."

"Oh, we're just friends," Gemma said with a modest giggle that implied a lot without actually saying it. As someone who'd never done any undercover work, Lucas was impressed at how seamlessly she was rolling with it. "We only met a few months ago."

He couldn't help but notice Gemma had the incredible ability to maintain her cover while also only saying things that were true.

"And what do you do?" Nicola asked.

"I own a bookstore in a small town in Northern Ontario," Gemma said, leaving out the fact that it was actually run by Jackson's fiancée, Amy.

"Did I hear you're a scientist?" Gemma asked.

The tone was light, but Lucas was positive the question came from somewhere deep within something she'd researched.

"Ha, no!" Nicola said. Her smile didn't fade but a faint and unmistakable hint of bitterness seeped into her tone. "I did get a scholarship to study engineering. But it was the kind that I had to reapply for each year and it vanished at the end of my first year when everybody found out my little brother was a notorious arsonist."

Lucas blinked. He hadn't known that.

But Gemma gasped and her eyes widened dramatically. "Oh wow! That's so unfair!"

Yeah, it was. And it put a fresh spin on both Pauly questioning if his connection to Robby had cost him a promotion and on Bea's persistent push to clear Robby's name. Did Robby's mother think clearing her son's name would also help Nicola and Pauly? Lucas glanced around. He didn't see Bea anywhere. Presumably Nicola and Robby's mother would've been invited. When he'd called earlier that morning, both Nicola and Pauly had been hard at work preparing for the party, but there'd been no mention of Bea.

Nicola waved a dismissive hand. "It's all ancient history," she said. "I dropped out of engineering, became a paramedic and never looked back."

"You're a doctor on wheels!" Gemma chirped. "That would explain the ambulance tire tracks in front of your house. I always wondered if ambulance drivers and firefight-

ers were allowed to borrow their vehicles on the weekend."
She laughed, self-consciously. "I watch a lot of crime shows."

Nicola blinked and stepped back.

"No," Nicola said and frowned, "those must be from my
husband's truck."

"Oh." Gemma's smiled didn't dim. "Silly me!"

Lucas's phone buzzed. He glanced at the screen to see
a text from Jackson that read 911 AT LIBRARY. Before he
could reply, his phone began to ring with a call from Caleb.

"One second," Lucas said, in what he hoped sounded like
a light and upbeat tone. He stepped away, pressed a finger
to his ear and answered. "Hey, Caleb."

"We need you at the library right away." Caleb sounded
worried and like he was in his truck. "Darcy's locked herself
in the basement. She's having some kind of mental breakdown and yelling that the room's on fire."

"Or maybe the room is actually on fire," Lucas said.

Phones began to ping and ring all over the backyard.
Gemma snatched her phone to her ear as she turned and ran
toward him. All over the barbecue, he watched as cops, firefighters and paramedics set down their burgers and punch
and started toward the front of the house.

"Michi, let's go!" Lucas summoned his partner to his
side as he turned and sprinted toward his SUV, trusting that
Gemma would keep up and join him. Last thing he wanted
was to risk getting slowed down by a crush of vehicles as
everyone tried to leave at once. "What do we know?" he
asked Caleb.

"Not much," the officer said. "People in the library heard
her banging on the door and screaming that there was a fire."

"Did she call 911?"

"No, other people did when they couldn't open the door."

Was she locked in? Lucas expected the basement didn't

have good enough phone reception for her to place the call herself.

"Also, crime scene investigators have searched her car, which was pulled from the lake, and found no evidence of an electronic device or detonator inside," Caleb went on. "Ditto at the school. So either Blaze used an arson device with no electronic components or the fire was set by someone who was there."

"In other words... Darcy." His stomach sank.

A second later, he reached the truck and threw the back door open, then Michigan jumped in.

"Lucas! Drive!" Gemma shouted. She sprinted around the side of the house with her phone to her ear, churning up gravel beneath her sandals, having shed every ounce of her party graces. "I'll meet you at the end of the driveway!"

"Got it!" He leaped in and started the engine. "Caleb, I'm on my way, I'll meet you there with Gemma."

"See you there." Caleb ended the call.

Quickly, Lucas navigated his truck through the maze of parked cars, aggressively pushing his bumper in front of other vehicles who were trying to get through, in a way he'd never normally dream of doing.

Gemma cut across the grass and met him at the end of the driveway. He leaned over and pushed the door open. She jumped in and slammed the door behind her.

"Jackson," she said into the phone, "I'm in the truck with Lucas. We'll be there in..."

Her voice trailed off as she looked to Lucas for the answer.

"Five minutes," he said. "Three and a half if I really push it."

"We'll be there in three," Gemma told her brother. "See you there." She ended the call and turned to Lucas in her seat. "Okay, here's what happened. A few minutes ago, people heard Darcy banging on the door and screaming to call 911 because there was a fire. The door was locked. Seems like she's also now somehow set the sprinklers off too. Fire-fighters, paramedics and cops were deployed. The building's being evacuated. I'm guessing she wasn't able to call 911 herself."

"Me too." Lucas swerved off around a corner and pressed the accelerator as quickly as he dared, praying he'd get there in time. "Caleb said apparently she was having some kind of nervous breakdown."

"That's an excellent theory," Gemma said, "but based on what I know of Darcy, I'm not sure it fits the facts. But Jackson did fill me in that investigators didn't find evidence of electronics or remote detonators during the previous incidents, which is another strike against her."

Lord, just please keep her safe until I get there.

She glanced at her phone. "It looks like they're deploying a full response just in case there is a fire."

Gemma pressed her lips together as if stopping a thought from leaving them.

"What?" he asked.

She sighed. "If Darcy is found alone, in a room that's on fire with the door locked seemingly from the inside, people are going to think she started it."

Traffic snarled to a standstill as he neared the library. Fire trucks, police and paramedics merged on the scene.

"Get out and run!" Gemma said. "I'll circle the block."

"Thanks." Lucas put the truck in Park and hopped out, calling for Michigan to join him. Michigan bounded up from the back seat and followed him out the front door moments before Gemma slid into the driver's seat.

Lucas ran down Main Street, weaving and dodging through first responders and civilians. Bright yellow police tape stretched along the pavement in front of the library, blocking his path. He leaped clean over it, with Michigan soaring by his side. Uniformed officers were ushering civilians away from the library. Other local cops blocked the front door. He didn't stop, just flashed his badge and ran through. The sound of an axe striking hard against wood sounded again and again from somewhere beneath them. Then came a splintering crash, followed by silence, and somehow the silence was most frightening of all. As he dashed down the narrow stairs leading to the reference room, he saw uniformed firefighters he knew well, standing, as if stunned, around the remains of a broken door.

As he approached, they moved aside.

"Hey, Lucas." A firefighter he'd known since kindergarten nodded toward him, respectfully but also a bit tentatively. "This chick's your friend, right? You want to handle this?"

Lucas glanced through the remains of the broken door. The room was drenched from the sprinklers above, which had destroyed the laptop, papers and files scattered across the research table. Darcy was crouched underneath with her hands wrapped around her knees.

Her chin rose as he met her tear-filled eyes.

"Yeah, I got this," Lucas said.

One of the firefighters patted him on the shoulder. "There was never any fire," he said, quietly. "She needs help."

Lucas nodded to show that he'd heard him. But his jaw clenched at the other man's flippant and disrespectful words. No doubt they were probably stepping back to help their fire chief's son avoid further embarrassment and he couldn't help but wonder what else local first responders might've ignored or swept under the rug to protect his father's reputation. Had any of these men seen Ed slipping on the job like Lucas had at home? He heard the firefighters shuffling away up the stairs, leaving him and Michigan alone in the hallway.

"It's not what it looks like," Darcy said.

"Okay," Lucas said. He stepped through the broken door. Carefully, Michigan jumped through after him. "I'm not even sure what it looks like."

"It was Blaze." Darcy's lips quivered like she was fighting the urge to scream and cry. "He said the final game starts tonight when the sun goes down. But I don't know where."

"What are you doing down there?"

"Avoiding the sprinklers," Darcy said. "I didn't want to get soaked."

"Michigan, search," Lucas murmured to his partner. Michigan began to sniff her way back and forth across the room. Then Lucas crouched until he was face-to-face with Darcy. "Talk to me."

"I don't know what to say," Darcy said. "I was alone in the room, researching every lead I could possibly think of. I gave the librarians a list of some fifty boxes of archives I wanted. Then suddenly, the door was locked, Blaze's voice was filling the room, telling me this was the final game and I was going to die. There was smoke. I saw flames."

She shrugged. Lucas glanced at Michigan for answers. His partner shook her shaggy blond head in frustration, like she wasn't sure if she detected something or not, because the residual scent was too faint.

"I started banging on the door and screaming for them to call 911," she went on. "I hopped up on a chair and set off the sprinklers with some matches I had in my purse. I heard commotion outside." She sighed and her shoulders drooped. "Then the flames and the voice vanished. They must've been illusions. Nothing more. The smoke was real, but the flames weren't. I'm guessing Blaze used a smoke bomb along with some kind of remote-controlled video projector. As a former STAV kid, that's what I'd have done, because they're pretty small and could be activated by someone standing outside the door. If it were me, I'd have smuggled them in inside one of the boxes. But I have no idea which one."

Lucas looked at Michigan again. The K-9 seemed to sense his need for answers and whimpered in response. It seemed his partner didn't have an answer for him one way or another.

Darcy took a deep breath and let it out.

"But this is good, right?" she added. "Because…because now we've got more information we can work with. Somewhere in this library is the answer to how he pulled this off… right? In fact, this might even explain how I saw Blaze inside my room when there was no evidence of a break-in." Confidence and doubt battled in her voice. "All I need is to find a way to dry all this out, get the laptop and cell phone repaired from water damage, and find, somewhere in this mess, whatever trick Blaze used to pull this off."

She sounded like she was trying to convince herself and she wasn't winning the battle. She slid out from under the table, and he reached for her hand to help her up to her feet. But she ignored it—if she even noticed it at all.

"I've just got to keep searching and I will find it," Darcy said. She stood and so did he. "I'm okay and I've got this."

His eyes flicked to the red and blue emergency lights flashing against the windowpane. She had no idea just how much the situation had spiraled out of anyone's control.

"Darce…" Lucas's voice dropped to a whisper. Her dark eyes met his. "You're not okay, and you've not 'got this.' But that's okay. My whole team is here for you. We can close down the crime scene, get forensics in here to go over every inch of everything in this room and get you somewhere safe where you can take a minute to breathe—"

A knock on the broken doorframe interrupted him mid-thought. They turned.

It was Corporal Austin Dillon. The man was practically puffing out his chest.

"Lucas, I need you to step out so I can talk to Darcy alone," Austin said.

Lucas felt the back of his neck bristle. Michigan growled under her breath.

"Thanks, Austin," Lucas said. "But we're good. Just let me handle it."

"K-9 Officer Lucas Harper," Austin commanded, his voice rising, "this is not a request. I am ordering you to vacate the scene, now!" Then he turned to Darcy as if Lucas didn't even exist. "Darcy Lane, I'm arresting you for criminal mischief, misleading a peace officer and misuse of emergency services."

"Don't be ridiculous," Lucas stepped between Darcy and Austin before she could even open her mouth to speak. "The Ontario Cold Case Task Force has authorization over all incidents relating to Blaze and this new copycat threat."

"Not anymore." Austin smirked. "The local chief of police contacted the Ontario police commissioner to object to your task force's sticking their nose in a local case and mucking it all up. You're protecting a criminal, who seems intent on causing chaos. And even your father, the fire chief, signed off on this."

She watched as Lucas winced. The corporal seemed to deliver that final blow about Ed with an extra hint of malice, just to twist the knife. Lucas glanced down at his phone.

"I need to call my boss, Inspector Ethan Finnick, to confirm he wants me to stand down on this," Lucas said. "Let's take the temperature down a few notches and go upstairs to get some fresh air so I can make a call somewhere with a cell phone signal."

"You can go wherever you want," Austin said, then gestured to Darcy, "but she's not going anywhere without handcuffs."

"Really?" Lucas asked. "You are power-tripping so hard right now, Austin."

In all the years she'd known Lucas, Darcy had never seen him that disgusted with another human being.

"We're not going anywhere," Lucas said. "Just give us five minutes. Then I'll go make my call."

Austin snorted. "And let you poison my witness's testimony?"

"You think anyone," Lucas started, "including me, is able to poison Darcy Lane's mind about anything? She's got the strongest, most stubborn mind I know."

Austin didn't respond for a long moment. Instead, the two men stared each other down as if waiting to see which one would blink first. In the end, it was Austin.

"Fine," Austin said. "I'll give you a couple of minutes out of professional courtesy to wrap up anything you need to for your own investigation. Then I expect you and your team to step away from this case."

He turned and clomped up the stairs, leaving Lucas, Darcy and Michigan alone again.

"Listen," Lucas whispered, turning toward her, "I don't trust him. But even if he's lying, it could take some time to sort out what the truth actually is. I've got to talk to Finnick. He'll have to follow this up the chain of command, and by that point Austin might have you sitting in a holding cell or interrogation room down at the main police station. Just remember, you have the right not to answer him and to ask for a lawyer."

Her mind was spinning and struggling to catch up with everything that was happening. Was she really about to be arrested?

"You've got to know that I have nothing to do with this Blaze copycat," Darcy said, "and I've never lied to you, about anything."

"I know." Lucas stepped forward. His voice was low, and his eyes looked intently into hers. His hands brushed her shoulders, and she could feel warmth and comfort spreading through her limbs from his touch.

"Hey, Lucas!" Austin shouted down from the top of the stairs. "You know, your new girlfriend is probably wondering where you are! I heard from the guys that she's driving up and down the street in your truck, trying to talk people into letting her into the cordoned-off area."

"Your girlfriend?" Darcy asked, pulling away from Lucas's touch. "What is he talking about?"

"Nothing," Lucas said, keeping his voice low so that Austin wouldn't overhear him, even if the corporal was trying to listen in. "I'm not in a relationship with anyone. He's just trying to start trouble. He's referring to Gemma. Finnick suggested that Gemma go undercover with me to Pauly and Nichola's long-weekend barbecue party," he said, "as a second pair of eyes. We told everyone she was just a friend who owns a bookstore up north."

"And the small-town gossips jumped to conclusions," Darcy said, filling in the blanks.

Yup, she got that. That made perfect sense. But still, it meant that Finnick had assigned Gemma to go to the party with Lucas, and Jackson to be the one who drove her around that morning. While Finnick and Lucas had spoken alone the night of the break-in, she'd reminded herself that while she could count on Lucas to do his job as a cop, she couldn't rely on him to be there for her as anything more than that.

She'd do good to remember that now.

Austin's voice rose, like he was baiting them to turn their attention back to him. "Gotta admit it's kind of pathetic to see two women fighting over a shoddy reject-cop who couldn't even get into his local police training." He laughed as he exited the basement.

Darcy waited for Lucas to brush off the obvious lie. But instead, she watched as he winced.

"Lucas?" She leaned toward him. "What's he talking about?"

He stepped back. "Nothing you need to worry about. I failed one major test, back when I was a teenager, which has nothing to do with my career now or this investigation."

"Maybe not," Darcy said. "I've been convinced that talking about the past will only make things worse. But by now I can also tell that ignoring it isn't making anything better. I can just tell that you're rattled right now, and I want to know why."

He closed his eyes, whispered a prayer and then opened his eyes again.

"I wasn't honest with you about why I moved out to B.C.," he said. "I don't know how Austin knows this, but I was rejected by the Ontario Police College. I knew for weeks that I was heading out West, but I didn't tell you and instead let you believe I was going to stay here. Even after you gave me that Ontario Police college sweatshirt and made plans for us to do things here in the fall. My self-esteem was so crushed. I was embarrassed and in denial, and didn't tell you. I'm sorry."

Darcy's whole body jolted like she'd just been slapped across the face with a cold, wet towel. She'd told and retold herself the story of what happened between her and Lucas, and that stupid kiss, hundreds of times over the years. And in none of the versions had it ever crossed her mind that he'd left because he'd been rejected by the Ontario Police College.

Or that he'd mislead her about it. Sudden heat rose to her face. She'd not only bought him that sweatshirt, he'd worn it for weeks.

"So, you knew you were about to fly to B.C. when you kissed me?" she asked.

"I did," he admitted. "I already had the ticket booked."

"Is what *why* you kissed me? Is that why you told me you loved me? Because you *knew* you were leaving and could just run away if you changed your mind?"

"No!" Lucas said. He rushed forward, closing the space between them. "I kissed you because I cared about you. And I told you it wouldn't work because I was sure that I'd only mess everything up. Especially as we'd be on opposite sides of the country."

She didn't even know what to say. She closed her eyes and tried to pray.

Be gentle and kind.

"I'm so sorry," Lucas said. "Are you angry?"

"I'm furious," she admitted. "I'm angry at you. But I'm also angry at me and at this whole situation. When all this kicked off, I just instinctively ran to you, without even stopping to think about what other options I had or what else I could do. I was one hundred percent certain that you were going to be the one to fix everything. Not because of your team. Not because you were a cop. But because something inside me was certain you were the one guy who I could count on above everyone else."

Her eyes opened. He was standing closer to her than she'd realized. Their feet were practically touching. If he'd tilt his head toward her or she stood up on her tiptoes, their lips might meet in a kiss again.

"Maybe you're not the hero I wanted you to be," she said, "but you're not the mess your father thinks you are either." She shrugged. "Maybe you're just a guy who doesn't always get it right."

And she couldn't just keep pretending that he was going to swoop in and save her.

She could hear Austin stomping back down the stairs now. She stepped back. So did Lucas.

"I'm going to go talk to Finnick," he said. "I'll go figure this out, and then someone will get in touch with you. To be honest, once Austin arrests you, I might have to keep my distance. Depending on the situation, I could be accused of trying to compromise his case or even threatened with losing my badge. You should also probably try to hire a lawyer."

She nodded. "You're probably right."

She could see Austin's feet and legs now as he came closer. She wanted Lucas to wrap his arms around her and guarantee that everything was going to be okay. But he couldn't. Maybe he'd never really been able to.

"I'm sorry I let you down," he said.

"I'm sorry too."

Then Lucas turned away, signaled Michigan to his side and together they disappeared up the stairs, leaving her alone with Austin.

The corporal stepped through the doorway. He loomed over her like a smug wolf sizing up a canary.

"Turn around," he ordered. "Hands up."

"Look, I'll go with you to the police station," Darcy said, "but you don't need to make it a whole thing."

His hand brushed the gun at his side, as if reminding her that there was nothing stopping him from pulling it.

"I said, turn around!" he bellowed. "Hands up."

"Okay!" Darcy raised her palms and turned back toward the table. Her heart was pounding in her chest more from indignation and frustration than from fear. She stared down at the wet papers melding together into a big soggy mess on the table. "Is this really necessary?"

He didn't answer. He just chuckled. It was an ugly sound.

Austin pulled her arms behind her back and held both wrists in one hand. Then she heard the jingle of handcuffs. She clenched her fingers into fists and felt the cold metal brush her skin as he clicked the handcuffs into place. To her embarrassment, she felt tears build up in the corners of her eyes.

No, she wasn't about to give him the satisfaction of crying in front of him.

Lord, help me. Please.

The grinning face of the Honey Bee Drive-In stared up at her from one of the soggy newspapers, reminding her of May long weekends spent sitting in the back of Lucas's truck and staring up at the big screen.

Hellllo, hoooney. Are you ready to have a fun and fabulous time?

Suddenly, a terrible certainty poured over her like ice water.

"Blaze is going to target the teen's event at the drive-in," Darcy exclaimed. "Tonight, when the sun sets and the movie starts!"

"Just shut up, okay?" Austin said. "Nobody is listening to your nonsense anymore."

He turned and propelled her up the stairs.

"No, you've got to listen to me," her voice rose. "I'm not making this up. Every time Blaze has called, he's said, 'Hello, honey,' and he told me the final game starts at sunset tonight. There's that huge event with all the teenagers. Someone needs to evacuate the drive-in immediately and search for an arson device."

It was all so clear. But how to get Austin to believe her before it was too late? He snorted and shoved her up the final step. She stumbled onto the library's main floor.

"Please!" Now her voice broke. "You've got to call it in right away! Blaze has threatened to set a fire at the drive-in. It's packed full of kids. All of them are in danger and could be killed!"

Desperately, she glanced from side to side. She didn't see Lucas or Michigan anywhere. In fact, she didn't see anyone anywhere, not even at the front door. The place had been completely cleared out. She'd just been researching Austin as a potential suspect. Was she alone with the Blaze copycat right now?

He steered her farther into the library.

"Where are we going?" she asked.

"I'm taking you out the back door," he said, "so you can't cause a further scene."

Desperation rose within her. But then how could she shout for help? How would anyone know that hundreds of locals were in danger?

"Listen to me!" she shouted. "Teenagers are going to die!"

"If you don't shut up, I'm going to muzzle you," Austin said. "All I've got to do is write in my report that you threatened to bite me."

He pushed her, just enough to make her lose her balance and knock her knee against a book cart, but not so hard he wouldn't be able to deny it.

That was it.

She relaxed her hands and felt her handcuffs loosen.

Help me, Lord, she prayed again.

She gritted her teeth, twisted her arms so hard her joints screamed in pain and swung her elbows high. Her left hand slipped free of its shackle. She elbowed Austin hard in the solar plexus, and he loosened his grip. Then she ran.

ELEVEN

She dashed down the library stacks, weaving between the tall and majestic rows of books and knocking carts over behind her. Austin was already giving chase. She could hear him behind her, swearing, yelling and ordering her to stop. He was a lot bigger and stronger than she was. But she had a small head start thanks to the element of surprise. She felt a breeze and followed it to the end of a row to find an open window. The glass pane had been pushed all the way to the top.

She leaped through, tumbled down a few feet and landed in a narrow alley between two buildings. She pressed herself against the rough brick wall and listened. There were lights and sirens to her right. To her left, traffic inched slowly down a side street as vehicles made their way around roadblocks. Behind her, she could hear Austin, in the library, looking for her and seemingly on the verge of losing it in anger.

Darcy ran down the alley toward Main Street, the handcuffs still dangling off one wrist. She wrapped her arm up in her sweatshirt to hide it. All she had to do was find somebody she trusted, someone who would take the threat of arson at the drive-in seriously. After that, she'd turn herself in to another cop and let them arrest her. And if she ended up sitting in a jail cell a long time for this, then fine. Just as long as she found someone who would ensure the teenagers were safe.

Lord, please help me find someone who will listen.

A flash of silver caught her eye from somewhere deep in the departing traffic that was moving away from her. A fresh breath of hope filled her chest, even as it ached with panic. It was Lucas's SUV. She ran for it down the center of the street, keeping her head low and using the vehicles on either side to shield her from view. She prayed that he'd see her and stop before traffic cleared ahead and he managed to pick up speed.

He was four cars away. Then two. Then three cars away again.

Traffic lurched forward.

"Lucas!"

The SUV stopped hard. Gemma's face leaned out the driver's-side window.

"Darcy!" she yelled. "Get in!"

The back door to the SUV swung open in front of her. Darcy leaped in and slammed it shut behind her.

"I think Blaze is going to target the drive-in tonight." Darcy crouched on the floor behind the driver's seat. "It's full of kids right now."

Gemma angled the rearview mirror to look back at her, just enough that Darcy could see her face in the corner.

"I'm guessing it was another riddle?" Gemma asked.

"Yeah."

"Good enough for me." Gemma typed a quick text into the phone on her dashboard. "I just texted Finnick that you think the drive-in is Blaze's next target. But I already know what he's going to say. Right now, I'm just doing circles around the area, waiting for Lucas to join me." Darcy noticed she hadn't texted Finnick about the fugitive in the back of Lucas's SUV. A second later, Gemma's phone beeped. The PI read the text out loud. "Yup. And he says to get Lucas. Get to the drive-in. Get proof. We can't risk another false alarm in case the real target's somewhere else."

"Did you learn anything interesting at the barbecue?" Darcy asked.

"Just that Nicola might've lost her university scholarship because of her connection to Robby."

Horns blared behind them, telling them to stop blocking traffic, and Gemma started rolling again.

"I thought you'd been arrested," Gemma said.

"I was."

Gemma eased the vehicle down a tight one-way street and pulled to a stop between two delivery trucks. "Okay, now we sit tight here and wait for Lucas," the PI said. "Did the arresting officer read you your full rights? All the way from 'I am arresting you for...' to 'You also have the right to apply for legal assistance through the provincial legal aid program'? I just like to know what level of crime I'm participating in."

Her blue eyes twinkled, and Darcy remembered what Jackson had said about her.

"No," Darcy said. "He didn't get that far. But he did handcuff me. It didn't take."

She held up the hand with the dangling cuff. Gemma shook her head and laughed.

"My brother said you reminded him of me," she said.

"He told me you don't like cops," Darcy said, "and yet you're on the Cold Case Task Force."

"He would say that." Gemma rolled her eyes. "That's an oversimplification. My view on law enforcement is a lot more nuanced than that. Basically, I think that if all cops were as good at listening to victims and responding to threats as the ones I work with, there'd be no cold cases." She grabbed a white daisy purse from in between the seats, which matched the flowers on her sundress, then tossed it back to Darcy. "There's a handcuff key in there. Also a small cell phone. Don't go anywhere without it."

"Thank you." Darcy found the key and, after a moment, worked her other hand free. Then she found the cell phone, switched it on and stuck it deep into her jeans pocket.

The back door slid open. Michigan leaped in on top of her and then woofed in surprise. She looked up from under the dog to see Lucas standing in the open door.

"Darcy?" His eyes widened. "What are you doing here?"

"Only a criminal-code violation 129," Gemma answered for her, "obstructing a peace officer." She shoved the driver's-side door open for Lucas and then slid into the front passenger seat. "Thankfully, he didn't read Darcy her rights, so it's not a 145, escape at large without an excuse."

Lucas winced like he'd developed an instant migraine.

"You should've been a lawyer," he told Gemma. He closed the back door and climbed in the front as Darcy detangled herself from the dog, sat up and put on her seat belt. "I'm also not sure you're right about the law. Finnick told me to make tracks to the drive-in and search it for an arson device. And I can't just take Darcy with me without committing a crime. Turns out, the Sunset police chief did send a strongly worded email to the commissioner of the Ontario Provincial Police, demanding that the Cold Case Task Force lose jurisdiction over this case immediately, and my father was one of the local leaders who signed off on it. The commissioner hasn't responded to it yet, which means Austin wasn't exactly telling the full truth. But I can't jeopardize the task force further by just running off with a fugitive."

"Lucas, listen—" Darcy started.

But he held up a hand. "Don't say anything!"

Then he turned around, reached between the seats and buckled Michigan's harness into a seatbelt. Then Lucas clasped a strong hand on Darcy's shoulder.

"Darcy Lane," he said, "I am arresting you for willfully resisting or obstructing a peace officer in the execution of his duty, which is a crime under the criminal code of Canada." Her stomach sank—what was he doing? "You have the right to retain and instruct counsel without delay. You also have the right to free and immediate legal advice from duty counsel by making free telephone calls..." He continued and, unlike Austin, covered every single word of her charter rights without missing a beat.

"Do you understand?" he concluded.

"Yes," she said.

That she was being arrested? Of course she did. Why Lucas was arresting her? No, definitely not. He sat back, sighed and started driving, out of downtown and toward the drive-in.

"Gemma," he said, "please inform Finnick by both text and email that I've arrested Darcy Lane on code 129 and she's now in my custody. I'm taking her to the scene of a potential crime as a material witness who may have relevant information. Make sure I'm copied on it and use every formal sounding word you think will cover all of our backs if someone tries to press the issue."

"Absolutely." Gemma pulled her phone from the mount on the dashboard and started typing. "Darcy, remember that now that you're under arrest, Lucas has the right to record anything you say and use it against you at trial."

She sounded like she was enjoying this, despite the very real tension that Darcy could sense all three of them were feeling.

"Now, we'll be at the drive-in in a couple of minutes," Lucas said. "What do I need to know? Was it a direct threat?"

Darcy took a deep breath. "No," she said. "But Blaze started almost every interaction by saying 'Hello, honey' in this long, theatrical, drawn-out way. Which reminded me of the Honey Bee Drive-In."

"And today's the first day it's open for the season," Lucas said before she needed to. "And it's packed full of kids. Gotcha."

He pulled out onto the road. They navigated through the mass of vehicles and pedestrians toward Main Street. Then suddenly Lucas slammed on the brakes so hard that all four of them were thrown forward. Darcy's shoulder strap cut into her shoulder and her stomach lurched. Cars squealed to a stop behind them. Michigan whimpered in protest.

She looked up through the windshield mirror to see a small, round woman with graying black hair and a cane, jaywalking slowing across the street and glaring at them through the windshield. Then Darcy immediately ducked down behind the seat.

Gemma asked. "What's up with her?"

"That's Bea Lamb," Lucas said. He blew out a hard breath. "Robby and Nicola's mom."

"Did she see me?" Darcy asked.

"I don't know," Lucas said. "I don't think so." He idled while she slowly made her way across the street. "I didn't know she had a cane."

"Neither did I." Darcy thought about the odd circular marks that Caleb had found. "Do you think it's possible she was lurking outside my house the other night?"

"Again, I don't know," Lucas said. "But we'll find out."

"I'm messaging Finnick about it now," Gemma said.

"The fact she's a couple of blocks from the library and

wasn't at the barbecue is already suspicious," Lucas said. "Once we clear the drive-in, we'll make sure one of us questions her."

Lucas waited until Bea was safely on the sidewalk, and then kept driving. Darcy sat back up in her seat. Minutes later he'd successfully cleared the traffic, navigated his way out onto a rural road and hit the gas.

"Now," Lucas said, "you were briefing me on why we're headed to the drive-in."

"Gemma had predicted there was a pattern to Robby's crimes," Darcy said. "Remember, I told you that the year before Robby started setting fire to buildings in downtown Sunset, he got really worked up about how the town was changing? It was like the edge of Toronto was trying to take over our small town, with big companies pushing out small businesses. Every place he hit fit the bill. The restaurant was a family place that was bought out by a corporate chain, which banned teenagers from coming in alone."

"I remember that," Lucas said. "The housing development was built in an area we used to bike as kids. The strip mall used to have the town's last game store."

"Exactly," Darcy said, thankful he was quick to keep up, "and the warehouse replaced an indoor play area. It doesn't begin to justify becoming a vigilante, but it might explain why."

"I also predicted there'd be a reason why the new copycat started up now," Gemma said.

"I don't know," Darcy admitted. "I still don't have an answer to that. But, Lucas, I did discover that your dad's first car accident was a lot more serious than you realized. I'm honestly surprised he's still alive, considering how bad it was. Maybe even more serious than Marie knew. Someone printed a picture of the crash in the local paper. The vehicle was completely totaled. But I'm guessing it was pulled, because it's not online."

"For all we know," Lucas said, "my dad had someone drive around town, collecting and destroying copies for him. But again, what that means for this case, I don't know."

They reached the drive-in. A line of vehicles waiting to get in snaked all the way down the road. Lucas drove down the hard shoulder, ignoring the indignant honks and yelling of teenagers who accused him of trying to cut the line. He parked as close to the entrance as he could and got out. Gemma, Darcy and Michigan followed, and they walked to an area overlooking the drive-in. The screens were set at the end of a winding road at the bottom of a natural valley. The design formed a triangle, with three large screens in opposite corners and a concession stand in the middle. Hundreds of cars were already parked in rows below them, waiting for the movie to start once the sun set. Maybe a thousand teenagers milled around the area—playing Frisbee and ball, eating food, and generally chilling with their friends—oblivious to the threat that when the sun went down, the entire place would go up in flames.

"It's like a giant firepit," Darcy said as she finally realized the full scale of the potential death and pain that Blaze was threatening to cause.

"There's only one way in and one way out," Gemma said, and for the first time since Darcy had met her, the private eye sounded genuinely scared. "The scale of this evacuation would be ten times what it was to clear the school. If we call this in, they evacuate all these kids and it's yet another false alarm, the reputation of our task force might never recover. Under the current circumstances, it could be the end of us. But I'm willing to risk it, if it means that otherwise all these kids are going to die. I can call in an anonymous tip to 911."

Lucas's face paled. Instinctively, Darcy reached for his arm, but he didn't even seem to feel her touch, so she pulled back.

"Okay," he said. "I'm going to get down there with Michigan and see if we can find the arson device—or devices—in time to get them deactivated before it's too late. Gemma, contact the team and get them to meet us here. I trust you on the 911 call."

"I can do it anonymously," Gemma confirmed, "and cancel it if you don't find anything. Also, I've already given Darcy a traceable phone, and I'll text you the number now."

"Thanks," Lucas said. "Now, let's all pray that the real threat isn't somewhere else and we risked a lot of lives by deploying resources to the wrong location."

He turned to Darcy, pulled his keys out of this pocket and reached out his hand to her.

"I need you to stay with the truck," he said. "Lock the doors and, in the worst-case scenario, you get somewhere safe."

"I won't leave without you," she said.

His fingers lingered on hers, not actually slipping through her hand, but not pulling away either. Lucas and Darcy stood there, with the tiniest bit of their bodies touching. And yet, as she looked in his eyes, she saw something unspoken there that went deeper than any hug or kiss they'd ever shared.

Finally, he pulled away. Wordlessly, they nodded to each other; then Darcy stood back and watched as Lucas, Michigan and Gemma ran down the long and winding driveway to the bottom of the hill. Lucas and Gemma split up at the bottom and went their separate ways. She soon lost sight of Gemma in the crowd. But Darcy kept watching as Michigan galloped up and down the rows of parked cars, with a determination and focus she'd never seen in the K-9 before.

Lucas's partner was on a mission, leaving him to run behind as the dog raced from vehicle to vehicle, searching for danger. Finally, she stopped at the back of a small hatchback, pressed her golden paws against the bumper and began to bark with such fury that even at a distance Darcy could hear its faint echo.

Michigan had found an explosive device. Rescue would be dispatched. It was all going to be okay. But then, as she watched, Lucas signaled Michigan to search again, and the dog took off running to another vehicle, and then another, barking at each. Her heart stopped. Just how many explosives devices were there?

As she jogged back to the SUV, she could hear the ping of texts and a chorus of voices groan as word spread between the cars full of teenagers who were still lining upon the road that according to their friends who'd already made it down into the event, a cop was running around the drive-in trying to get people to leave.

"They say there's an explosive device," a bored male voice floated from one car. "I don't believe it. It's probably just another false alarm. I'm just going to sit here and wait."

A chorus of voices from other cars agreed. Sirens began to sound in the distance. Darcy looked back down toward the drive-in to see a logjam of vehicles trying to leave while others blocked their path, refusing to back up and lose their place in line. What was more worrying was the number of teenagers who were just continuing to eat food or play games.

Her own words to the Cold Case Task Force echoed in the back of her mind.

Hoax calls are dangerous. The problem with false alarms is that then people stop taking real threats seriously. Especially teenagers. Too many false alarms in a given year, they'll just start assuming all emergency evacuations are fake. They'll shuffle their feet as slowly as possible or even just hide in a bathroom or closet and wait it out.

Her lungs tightened in her chest.

There had to be something she could do. After all, she talked panicked teenagers safely through emergencies every day at her job. Simon had told her the STAV teenagers had been posting about her rescuing them online.

Help me, Lord. Guide me.

She yanked the phone that Gemma had given her out of her pocket and dialed the drive in.

"Hello, National Drive-In, Sunset location," the voice was male and sounded tired. "Carter speaking."

The name rang a bell in the back of Darcy's mind. Thankfully she remembered why.

"Carter," she said. "You're Brittany's boyfriend, right? You both work at the drive-in? Is she there."

"Yes," he sounded confused. "But she's on the grounds. Is this Brittany's mom?"

Darcy took a deep breath.

"I'm the 911 dispatcher that Brittany talked to when you had your accident with the pill the other day," she said. She heard him gasp. "I'm also the one who you've probably seen online helping the high school kids during the fire. I need you to know that the evacuation call you just got is extremely real. You've got to get everyone out of there. There are multiple explosive devices. There will be a fire in the drive-in. People will be hurt."

"Oh, wow." There was a shuffling noise as if Carter put his hand over the phone. "Hey guys!" he called. "It's the 911 lady who saved my life. She says we gotta get everyone out of her. There's going to be a fire for real."

Then his voice was back on the phone. "Why are you calling to tell me that?"

"Because some kids don't believe the threat is real," she said, "but they'll listen to their friends."

"Yeah," he sounded shaken, but focused. "Brittany's got a big social media. And I'll tell people to message everyone they know. Bye and thanks."

The call ended and Darcy exhaled. Within moments she could hear the pings of cellphones around her—some others actually ringing—and voices shouting that the drive-in social media account had posted in all caps that everyone had to clear out. Horns were honking. Vehicles were turning around. Word was getting out.

Thank You, God. Everything was going to be okay.

She jogged back down the road toward Lucas's SUV.

Suddenly, a burst of smoke and flame filled the air in front of her, the blast knocking her backward off her feet as heat singed her skin. Her head smashed against the ground. Darkness filled her gaze.

A soft hand touched her body.

"Hey, Darcy." Blaze's voice was an odd and distorted whisper. She looked up, but all she saw was a figure shrouded in a hood. Something sharp pricked her arm, sending pain coursing through her body. "You're not going to win this game."

Fear crushed Lucas's heart like a vise as he looked up the hill to see his own SUV burning like a ball of flames against the afternoon sky.

Darcy!

He'd told her to stay at his vehicle because he'd wanted to keep her safe. Instead, she might be gone forever, and it was all because of him.

For a moment, he stood frozen, wanting to run to her but unable to get his legs to move. Then he felt his K-9 butting her head hard against the back of his knees, propelling him to run.

Lucas clipped Michigan's leash to her K-9 vest, wrapped his hand around it tightly and let his partner help pull him up the hill, back toward his SUV. He reached the top and sprinted down the road toward the fire.

"Darcy!"

Her name tore through his chest and out his mouth as if ripping his heart in two on the way. He was vaguely aware of voices shouting and sirens blaring. But all he could see was the heavy black cloud of smoke rising from his SUV, punctuated by bright orange flames. He ran straight for it. There was a tug on the leash, and Michigan fell back, trained to keep a safe distance from fire without a direct order. Lucas dropped the leash and surged on. The smell of ash and burning fuel filled his throat. Searing air stung his skin. The earth seemed to radiate heat through the soles of his boots.

Then he felt one strong pair of hands grab him by the right shoulder and another by the left, pulling him backward before he could plunge his body right into the blaze.

"Lucas, it's okay!" Caleb said, and Lucas realized he was on his right and Finnick was on his left. "She's not there. She's not in the car. We've already checked. We think she'd been kidnapped."

Kidnapped?

Caleb's voice was calm and steady. But still Lucas felt like the world was about to tip beneath his feet.

"Hey!" Finnick slapped his shoulder, like his coach used to before a particularly hard play. "I've been there, and I have some idea of what you're feeling right now. But you can't let despair win. Darcy's gone, and we need your head in the game if we're going to find her."

Lucas closed his eyes and breathed a prayer for Darcy's

protection. It came from somewhere so deep inside him that he couldn't even put it into words. His boss and colleague let him go. Together the three men stepped back from the fire, and once again he felt Michigan move to his side.

"Jackson and Hudson have tracked Darcy's scent down the road," Finnick went on. Like Caleb, his boss was keeping his words quick, level and calm. "They lost her scent there. We think that when the explosive went off in your car, she was dragged to another vehicle. Gemma was able to track her cell phone a few miles before it switched off, presumably because whoever abducted her found and destroyed it."

Law enforcement, paramedics and firefighters poured onto the scene to battle Lucas's flaming SUV, disarm the arson devices Michigan had detected and search for others, and evacuate everyone on the scene. The sheer scale of the operation was overwhelming, and Lucas imagined local law enforcement would have to bring in reinforcements from the surrounding area. Especially if the arson devices at the drive-in started exploding before everyone got out. Within moments, Gemma and Jackson had jogged back from opposite directions and joined the group. The five members of the team and the three canines moved to the side of the road, farther away from the burning SUV.

"Let's all accept as given that Darcy has been kidnapped and is in danger for her life," Finnick said. "How do we find her? Suggestions?"

"Obviously, we canvass the area for witnesses who might've seen the kidnapping," Caleb said, and shrugged. "But in this chaos, it could take hours to find a solid lead, even if our potential witnesses weren't being ordered to evacuate the scene."

"Our electronic-surveillance capabilities are also extremely limited," Gemma said. "When I lost the signal, they were driving into the woods along the shore of Lake Simcoe. We're talking very few, if any, cameras. The best we can hope for is that some residents have security cameras in front of their homes."

"Search and rescue is limited too," Jackson said, and sighed. "Gigantic amount of ground to cover, thick forests with rivers and lakes. Not to mention heavy tree cover blocking search by air. It would take a full-scale response."

"And that's going to be tricky for us to mobilize reinforcements and pull in any favors right now," Finnick said, "especially if it means convincing them our missing prisoner has been kidnapped."

"You mean, I messed up," Lucas said. "When I arrested her, I was trying to protect her and protect the team. But instead I might've killed us both."

He could feel the blood suddenly rush from his face. He felt sick. It was like all this time he'd been walking along a narrow ledge, trying to make sure every step he took was perfect, trying not to fall. And now he'd slipped, he'd failed and was tumbling into nothingness below. He'd failed Darcy. He'd failed his team. He was the failure his father had always told him he was destined to be.

"Hey!" Caleb stepped in front of his face and snapped his fingers. "I can see where your mind is spinning. Snap out of it. You think you're the first person to ever make a mistake on this team? I let a killer escape justice because of my own stupid feelings. Jackson here pretended to be Finnick to lie to a girl. Gemma practically faked her own death, and Finnick..."

Caleb's voice trailed off as Finnick stepped forward and put a hand on Caleb's shoulder.

"This is why we don't put Caleb in charge of PR," Finnick said, mildly. "Needless to say, I've got fifteen to twenty years on most of you. That's plenty of time to make mistakes, and I'm not going to stand around listing them now. All that matters is how we're going to find Darcy. And that means we've each got to dig deep, think, pray, and figure out what we've got to work with and who we can call." He glanced at Lucas. "And no more beating yourself up. In my experience, trying to get everything right gets in the way of hearing what God wants you listening for."

Lucas swallowed hard and nodded. "Thanks."

Then he closed his eyes.

Thank You, God, for this team. Please keep Darcy safe. Help me hear what You need me to hear. Help us find her.

He hadn't realized just how much, in his panic, he'd tuned out the noise and chaos of the scene around him. But it was all rushing back to him, like someone had turned up the volume of the world around him. Sirens, shouting, the sounds of people evacuating—and then, above it all, the loud, long and almost obnoxious honking of fire trucks, sounding like giant red geese ordering everyone around them to clear a path.

One commanding voice suddenly rose above them all.

He could hear his dad. Lucas's eyes snapped open.

"I'm going to talk to Ed," he said. He turned to Michigan. "Find Dad! Where's Dad?"

Michigan woofed and sniffed the air. She may not have anywhere near the skills of a search and rescue K-9 like Hudson, but she was still a huge help when it came to finding someone she knew. Lucas weaved in between the fire trucks and vehicles, asking firefighters if they'd seen the chief.

Then, finally, he saw his father stepping out of the passenger side of a large white fire department SUV.

"Dad!" Lucas ran toward his father. "We need to talk. Darcy's been kidnapped."

Genuine worry and confusion filled his father's face.

"I'm so sorry," Ed said. His father's hand touched his shoulder, and suddenly Lucas remembered how comforting it had been as a kid in those moments he knew his dad was there for him. "What happened? Is she okay?"

"I don't know," Lucas said. "Someone grabbed her, and I'm sure it was Blaze." He swallowed hard. "Dad, I know you don't want to talk about Robby Lamb or Blaze, let alone why you've decided to stay in a hotel instead of with me—"

"Enough!" Ed barked. His grip suddenly went hard as instantly the care disappeared from his eyes, replaced with frustration, bordering on anger, like a switch had been flipped. "Come on, son! Now is not the time or place to bring all that up!"

"I know!" Lucas stepped backward and threw both of his hands up. "Harper men don't air their dirty laundry in public. Let alone in the middle of a chaotic law enforcement operation. But if it's any comfort, I don't think anyone cares about our family squabbles right now or is trying to listen in on our conversation."

Ed waved his hands as if telling Lucas to stop. But Lucas wasn't about to be halted. Not this time. Not with Darcy's life in danger.

"You just keep giving me the exact same brush-off over and over again," Lucas continued. "Ever since I came back into your life, you've refused to talk me—about your car accidents, or moving into a bungalow, or Marie leaving, or any of it. But for what it's worth, Darcy saw pictures of your original accident and says she's surprised you even survived."

"Son, drop it," Ed warned.

"Now I've found out you signed onto this letter trying to revoke my task force's jurisdiction on the Blaze case," Lucas plowed on. "Why? What have I ever done to you to make you hurt me like that? And why won't you just tell me about your conversation with Robby Lamb and how you got him to confess he was Blaze?"

"Because I don't remember," Ed muttered, angrily.

"You don't remember why you sabotaged my career, won't help find Darcy, won't help stop Blaze—"

"I don't remember talking to Robby Lamb!" Ed snapped.

And while his father's voice was barely audible in the sea of noise surrounding them, to Lucas, it cracked the air like a whip. For the first time in his life, Lucas saw pain and helplessness flood his father's eyes. Gently, he put his hand on his dad's shoulder and steered him away from the scene to the very edge of the crowd.

"What do you mean, you don't remember?" he asked, softly.

"I got what they call a TBI from my first accident." Ed sounded disgusted and frustrated by it. "It impacts my ability to remember stuff and get words out right."

"You have a traumatic brain injury?" Lucas said. Pain filled his heart. "Dad, I'm so sorry. Those are serious. You can't drive—"

"You think I don't know that?" Ed barked. But now, for the first time, Lucas didn't think he was actually upset at Lucas but at the situation or himself. "That's why I moved into the bungalow and then the hotel, so I didn't have to drive to work. As for Marie, I don't even know what I said that got her so upset to make her leave. Sometimes my tone and words are off. But I didn't want to worry her, or you, for any of this."

Understanding dimmed slowly in Lucas's mind. Way back at the beginning, Finnick had instructed them all to second-guess their own preconceived ideas about this case.

He'd never even questioned that his father could help them but was just choosing not to.

"So, you honestly didn't recognize Blaze's voice on that 911 call," Lucas said, slowly.

"No, I didn't," Ed admitted. "I also don't remember enough about Robby or the case to help your team and didn't remember you were part of that task force when I was asked to sign the letter about outsiders interfering in local law enforcement business. I've got memory gaps."

Ed sighed. Frustration, understanding and pity battled in Lucas's core.

Was this how he'd come across to Darcy when he'd asked her not to tell his colleagues that he'd been overpowered by Blaze?

Lord, next time I'm tempted not to admit my weaknesses or ask for help, please remind me just how dangerous that can be.

"Dad, you can't go on like this."

"Look, I'm less than a year away from retirement," Ed said, bristling. "There's no reason for me to be forced out of my job. I just figured I'd ride it out until the end, retire on a full pension and nobody had to know."

Except the one criminal whom Ed had gotten to confess was somehow back. And if someone used this new copycat to clear Robby's name and reopen the case into Blaze being Robby, he wouldn't be able to testify to anything Robby had said.

In fact, the only people who could possibly testify against Robby were Ed and Darcy.

One of whom had a brain injury and the other of which was gone.

Gemma had predicted there'd be a reason why these new copycat crimes had started up now. What if the copycat was someone who knew about Ed's traumatic brain injury? What if the copycat's whole game had been about making Darcy look unreliable and making sure that nobody believed her or Ed?

What if it had all been about clearing Robby's name, just as Bea had been fighting for?

Lights and sirens flashed around them. Terrible clarity washed over him like rain.

"Dad? Who knows about your traumatic brain injury?"

"No one," Ed said, and shook his head in frustration. "Except for a couple of doctors and the crime scene paramedics."

His heart stopped. "Which ones?"

TWELVE

A blinding light suddenly jolted Darcy's brain back into consciousness. She blinked, but the light was so bright that all she could see was red inside her lids.

"Darcy, tell me why you first suspected that Robby was Blaze," a disembodied voice floated from somewhere to her right.

She seemed to be sitting up on some kind of folding bed. She tried to sit up straight. Tight straps wrapped around her stomach and wrists were holding her in place.

She couldn't move.

"Who are you?" Darcy asked. "Where am I?"

No answer came but the buzz of the lights and the electronic droning of some kind of machine she couldn't see.

"I don't want to hurt you," the copycat's voice was soothing now—gentle, even. "But I'll zap you again if you struggle or fight me. Just start talking about Blaze and Robby, and I'll tell you when to stop."

She tried to stretch but found another strap holding her legs down.

Darcy closed her eyes as tightly as she could.

Help me, Lord. I'm trapped and I'm terrified.

She needed time to figure out where she was. She needed to give Lucas and his team time to find her. She heard a click and realized she was probably being recorded by her captor. But the copycat wasn't giving her a script. Gemma's words floated through her mind: *You can make a computer-generated deepfake of anybody's voice with a large enough sample size.*

Just start talking, Darcy, and trust that help is on the way. Be gentle and kind.

And keep talking.

"I'm sorry I didn't do more to help Robby Lamb when he was alive," Darcy said.

"Really?" Blaze said.

"Yes." Darcy opened her eyes and stared at the gray edges of the block of blinding light filling her gaze. *Lord, help me adjust to the light.* "Robby wasn't some unfeeling monster set on destruction. He cared really deeply about what happened to our town."

"Yeah." The Blaze distortion dropped, just enough that Darcy could hear a second voice now, female and sad, leaking through. There was a creaking sound, like Darcy's captor was sitting down on a chair. Then the voice distortion slipped completely, and for the first time, Darcy heard the true voice of the person who'd been tormenting her all along. "Maybe too deeply."

Nicola.

The paramedic.

And Robby's big sister.

"I know," Darcy admitted. "He hated to see the direction the town was going. And I think every single target that he went after was something he loved about this town that he watched disappear in front of his eyes. Like a restaurant, or game store, or biking trail."

The light seemed to have shifted slightly to the right when Nicola sat. Now she could see a faint outline of the space.

Darcy was strapped to a gurney in the back of an ambulance. A large spotlight shone in front of her. A video camera was locked on her face. The back doors were open. Darkness had fallen, but she could hear the rustle of wind in the trees and water lapping against the shore. Then she glanced to her side and saw more recording equipment, medical devices, a smoke machine and a video projector.

"Yeah." Nicola sighed, slowly. Darcy turned toward her. Her figure was swamped in the gigantic sweatshirt disguise that her younger brother had used to commit his crimes.

"I could've listened," Darcy said. "I could've noticed he was in trouble sooner and tried to get him help. But I couldn't have saved him. Because I was just a kid, and he needed way more serious help than I could provide."

She took a deep breath and felt tears prick the corners of her eyes, which had nothing to do with the light shining on her.

"And you couldn't have rescued him either, Nicola," Darcy said. She heard a soft gasp. "You were also just a teenager. He needed professional help. Nobody saw it and he was failed by a lot of people. He also made his own choices, as terrible as they were. And your whole family has been paying for it, in one way or another, ever since."

"My mother is convinced he was innocent," Nicola said. "She says that he never got a fair trail because Ed talked him into confessing and turning himself in. Mom says Ed's the reason that Robby is dead and that Paul was turned down for his promotion."

"And that you lost your scholarship, right?" Darcy asked. "Your mom was the one who set up the projector inside the library today, wasn't she? And the one who projected Blaze in through the crack of my bedroom window. It was very convincing."

Nicola didn't answer. But she also didn't argue.

"Framing me for your brother's crimes won't heal your mom's pain or change your family's life," Darcy said. "Discrediting Ed's memory won't either. No matter how sophisticated a confession tape you construct or how cleverly you dispose of my body—even if you somehow manage to clear Robby of the crimes you know he committed—it won't give you peace. I don't know what it feels like to be you, but I know ignoring the truth didn't help me, and I'm sure it won't help you."

And, Lord, if I don't make it out of here alive, please give Lucas the reassurance that I love him, I forgive him and I'm sorry.

The angry buzz of a stun gun sounded in her ear. She clenched her jaw and braced herself for the pain.

"Darcy!" A deep and strong voice, that every part of her heart would always know, cut through the night along with the sound of a dog barking. "Darcy, can you hear me?"

"Lucas!" she screamed with every ounce of energy she had. "I'm here!"

"Shut up!" Blaze's voice was suddenly back. The light switched off, plunging Darcy into darkness again. There was a flurry of activity around her as Nicola seemingly switched the camera off. A lighter clicked. Then a bright orange flame flickered in front of Darcy's eyes. "Or I'll light you up and set this whole place alight with you inside."

"Darcy?" Lucas's voice sounded again in the distance. "Guys, I thought I saw a light in the trees, but it's gone now. Let's go back the other way."

He didn't know where she was. He didn't know how to find her.

He wasn't going to find her in time.

Unless she risked getting burned by the flames.

"Lucas!" Darcy screamed. "I'm here! Blaze is Nicola!"

For a moment, it was like time stopped as she watched the bright orange flame fall out of view. Then she felt a rush of fire and smoke engulf her. *Save me, Lord!* Darcy screamed and thrashed her body from side to side. Her legs fell free. A hand smacked her hard across the face. But she kicked up hard, sending Nicola flying backward. Nicola hit the wall, groaned and crumpled to the floor.

The legs of the gurney collapsed beneath her, sending her body falling straight down three feet to the floor, knocking the air from her lungs. Fire rose on either side of her. Darcy kicked out at the projector, trying to hit the button with her heels.

"Hellllo, hoooney," Blaze said. "Ready to play another game?"

Suddenly, a projection of Blaze loomed above her in the darkness, exactly the same way he'd appeared in her bedroom in the middle of the night, only now the figure was gigantic and over three stories tall as it bounced off the smoke and trees.

"Hello again, Darcy," Blaze's distorted voice droned on. "Did you miss me? You do like solving riddles, don't you, Darcy? You think you're smart, with your little mind whirring away, figuring things out."

"She's over here!" Lucas shouted. "Darcy, I'm coming!"

Suddenly, like a comet in the darkness, she saw Michigan leaping toward her through the flames. Then Lucas reached her side. In an instant, he'd cut her loose from the gurney and gathered her up into his arms.

"Way to signal for help, Darce." He cradled her tightly to him, and she could feel his cheek against hers. "But I am going to carry you right now—don't fight me on this."

A laugh slipped from her lips, mingled with a sob. "I won't."

He ran out of the flaming ambulance with Darcy in his arms and Michigan at his side.

"Nicola's still in there," Darcy said. "I think I might've knocked her out."

But just as the words were leaving her mouth she saw Caleb, Jackson and his K-9 partner, bursting through the forest toward them.

"Nicola's still in the ambulance," Lucas called. "She might be injured. Get firefighters out here. I'm going to take Darcy to safety."

"Head for the water!" Caleb called back. "The wind is going to blow the fire straight back toward the road."

"Will do!" Lucas turned and ran through the trees toward the sound of water.

"Nicola is Blaze," Darcy said.

"We know," Lucas said. "Or, as Finnick would say, we suspected pretty hard and compiled enough corroborating evidence to obtain an arrest warrant for kidnapping."

She looked over her shoulder and back. Fire crackled behind. Darkness filled the woods ahead of them. But for the first time in a long time, there was a lightness in Lucas's voice.

"A lot's happened since you vanished," he said. "I yelled at my dad, and he admitted he had a traumatic brain injury that had been messing with his mind. He wasn't sure, but he thought Nicola might've been one of the paramedics who treated him. Then we pulled both Pauly and Bea in for questioning. Caleb got Pauly to confess that Nicola had been disappearing at odd hours of the night and confirmed Gemma's suspicions that she'd brought the ambulance to their house, against orders. He gave Gemma access to her computer and agreed to help us find her. When Finnick challenged Bea, she broke down and confessed to helping Nicola, in the hopes of finally getting Robby's name cleared."

The trees parted ahead of them. Night sky filled her gaze.

"Now, hang on tight," he said, "because I'm about to jump."

Darcy buried her head into his neck. Lucas's arms tightened around her. Then she felt him leap into nothingness. For a moment, they fell together into the unknown. Then she felt their bodies hit water, and Michigan splashed into the lake beside them. Lucas let her go, and together they swam to a rock jutting out of the water, crawled up and sat, side by side, looking back at the flames.

"Believe it or not, we're only about a fifteen-minute walk from where you crashed your car into the lake," he said. "We didn't find any signs of electronic explosives in the Matthews' garage. It looks like she only used common household things that would vanish without a trace, like chlorine tablets and lighter fluid."

That would explain why she'd smelled chlorine in her car and the school, and why crime scene investigators hadn't found any electronics.

"Then I'm guessing she didn't use a precision timer," Darcy said, and shivered. "She just set it up ahead of time and let it slowly drip until it burst into flame."

Thank You, Lord, that Nicola was stopped before anyone else was hurt.

Quickly, Darcy told Lucas everything that had happened in the ambulance between her and Nicola, and he filled her in on his end of the investigation.

"So, when Nicola discovered Ed wouldn't be able to back up Robby's confession she created a copycat Blaze in the hopes of getting the initial investigation reopened," Darcy said. "Then when I got involved, she saw her opportunity to get revenge on me too, and Bea was only too happy to help."

"No wonder you were afraid when Blaze appeared in your room," Lucas said. "That giant Blaze projection was terrifying."

Michigan shook the lake water from her fur, showering them with it, then collapsed at their feet.

Lucas laughed and wrapped his arm around Darcy, and she leaned into him. He placed a quick call to his team and confirmed that everyone was fine and out of the fire's path. They'd emerged from the forest a little farther down the shore and were now waiting in the water for evacuation.

Firefighters and helicopters were on their way.

"I'm surprised you got Pauly to hand over his wife's computer," Darcy admitted.

Lucas shrugged; then his arm tightened around her.

"He really loves her," Lucas said, "and I think he's willing to forgive her and stand by her while she goes to jail, if that's what she wants."

"I hope so," Darcy said, "for her sake. Does that sound weird, considering everything she's done to us?"

"No, it doesn't," Lucas said. "I think, under all that fight, you've got the biggest heart of anyone I've ever met."

For a long moment, she stared up at the bright orange flames as they licked against the night sky. Then his fingers brushed along the side of her face, pulling her toward him. His nose brushed against hers.

"I'm sorry I ever let you think I wasn't in love with you," he whispered. "I wasn't ready to be with you back when we were younger. But that didn't mean I didn't love you. I've always loved you, Darcy."

"I've always loved you too," Darcy whispered back. "Am I still under arrest?"

Lucas chuckled. "No."

"Good," she said. "Then I won't get in trouble for doing this."

She wrapped her arms around the neck of the man she loved and kissed him, without a hint of reservation or doubt in her mind.

Lucas pulled her closer and kissed her back. Suddenly, he stopped.

"You're going to marry me, right?" he asked.

She laughed. "Absolutely."

"Good," he said. "Because you're so much more than I've ever dreamed of finding."

He kissed her again, and she relaxed into his arms, knowing that whatever battles life threw at them next, they'd always fight together.

* * * * *

If you enjoyed this story,
find other pulse-pounding reads in the
Unsolved Case Files series from
USA TODAY *bestselling author*
Maggie K. Black.
Available now from
Love Inspired Suspense!

Dear Reader,

Sometimes when I write a book, I know who the characters are before I start. That was definitely true with Finnick, Casey, Jackson and Amy when they walked onto the pages of the first two books in the Unsolved Case Files stories.

But other times, they sneak up on me as I tell their story.

Darcy was one of those characters that snuck up me. The more I wrote about her, the more she reminded me of myself. As a teenager, I valued my faith and doing the right thing so incredibly highly. Yet there were so many times I know I thoughtlessly hurt others by letting my thoughts and feelings just spill out of me like an uncontrollable fire.

Our words and stories are powerful. Thank you for picking up this book and giving me the opportunity to try to use my words for good. And my prayer is that God will guide you in how you share your words and voice in the world around you.

To those who've asked, the dog I mentioned in *Cold Case Trail* is still doing a wonderful job of causing delightful chaos in my life.

Thank you again for sharing this journey with me,

Maggie